Drew spent most of his professional life working in the Engineering Design Services sector, managing sophisticated three-dimensional software applications. It was a challenging and demanding environment and upon retirement his eldest daughter suggested that he went back to what she as a child loved best, which was Drew telling her stories completely unaided and straight out of his head. Never declining a challenge, Drew started writing a few months prior to his retirement and found the stories just tumbling out quicker than he could write them. Drew admits that this was and still is a most rewarding and creative experience that anyone could possibly want to pursue.

I would like to thank my family and especially my dear, long-suffering wife, Sophie for reading and listening to the story proofs. Also, to my daughters Claire and Victoria, for being part of my story's inspiration.

Drew Salah

The Adventures of Harry Alliss (and Friends)

Austin Macauley Publishers™
LONDON * CAMBRIDGE * NEW YORK * SHARJAH

Copyright © Drew Salah 2022

The right of Drew Salah to be identified as author of this work has been asserted by the author in accordance with sections 77 and 78 of the Copyright, Designs and Patents Act 1988.

All rights reserved. No part of this publication may be reproduced, stored in a retrieval system, or transmitted in any form or by any means, electronic, mechanical, photocopying, recording, or otherwise, without the prior permission of the publishers.

Any person who commits any unauthorised act in relation to this publication may be liable to criminal prosecution and civil claims for damages.

A CIP catalogue record for this title is available from the British Library.

ISBN 9781398458505 (Paperback)
ISBN 9781398458512 (Hardback)
ISBN 9781398458529 (ePub e-book)

www.austinmacauley.com

First Published 2022
Austin Macauley Publishers Ltd®
1 Canada Square
Canary Wharf
London
E14 5AA

To David Blackford, for creating the wonderful illustrations for Harry Alliss

Table of Contents

Book One   13

Harry and the Secret Garden   15

   Chapter One – The Voice   15

   Chapter Two – In the Space Station   23

   Chapter Three – Homeward Bound   27

   Chapter Four – The Explanation   31

   Chapter Five – Did It Ever Happen?   33

Harry and the Ill Little Girl   35

   Chapter One – Going to Hospital   35

   Chapter Two – Meeting Ellie and Lady Vix   37

   Chapter Three – The Breakfast   41

   Chapter Four – The Return Visit   44

   Chapter Five – What to Do?   46

Harry, Aunty Dare and Her Magical Motor Scooter   48

   Chapter One – Aunty Dare   48

   Chapter Two – The Magical Tour   53

   Chapter Three – Back Home   59

Harry and the Bad Neighbour   60

   Chapter One – Harry Having a Think   60

   Chapter Two – Neighbours   62

   Chapter Three – The Accident   66

   Chapter Four – The Ambulance Arrives   69

   Chapter Five – The Home Coming   72

Harry and the Train Ride   **75**

Chapter One – Catching the Train   *75*

Chapter Two – The Wizard   *79*

Harry and the Lightning Pilot   **84**

Chapter One – The Robbery   *84*

Chapter Two – Meeting Roy   *87*

Chapter Three – The Test Drive   *90*

Harry and the Boy in the Tree   **95**

Chapter One – Difficult Times   *95*

Chapter Two – The Boy in the Tree   *97*

Chapter Three – The Discovery   *102*

Book Two   **105**

Harry and the New Puppy   **107**

Chapter One – Who Wants a Dog?   *107*

Chapter Two – Finding a Dog to Love   *109*

Chapter Three – The Fair   *113*

Chapter Four – Pluto to the Rescue   *115*

Chapter Five – The Round Up   *119*

Harry and the Little Boat   **121**

Chapter One – The Breakthrough   *121*

Chapter Two – Mr Riggley-Sey   *124*

Chapter Three – The Holiday Drama   *126*

Chapter Four – All's Well   *131*

Harry and Santa Claus   **132**

Chapter One – The Christmas Turkey   *132*

Chapter Two – Santa Arrives   *135*

Chapter Three – An Amazing Day   *139*

Chapter Four – Total Fun Day   *144*

Harry and the Scout Camp   **145**

Chapter One – Hugo's Scout Camp Idea	145
Chapter Two – The Fireside Scout Hall Meeting	147
Chapter Three – Off to the Scout Camp	151
Chapter Four – The Adventure Trek	153
Chapter Five – The Rescue	158
Chapter Six – Going Home	160

Harry and All at Sea — 162

Chapter One – Planning a Holiday	162
Chapter Two – The Upset	167
Chapter Three – The Island	168
Chapter Four – Mission Control	171
Chapter Five – Meeting Soraya	172
Chapter Six – The Rescue Pilot	175
Chapter Seven – Roy Bankstead at Your Service	178
Chapter Eight – Are We Dreaming?	183
Chapter Nine – The Press Outside	184

Harry and the Grand Prix Races — 186

Chapter One – The Invitation	186
Chapter Two – Going to the Races	188
Chapter Three – The Practice	193
Chapter Four – The Bad Sport	196
Chapter Five – Angry Henry	198
Chapter Six – Before the Race	199
Chapter Seven – The Race	201
Chapter Eight – Closing Up	204

Harry and the Mighty Grunge — 206

Chapter One – An Early Morning Start	206
Chapter Two – Finding the Computer	208
Chapter Three – Where Is Aunty Dare?	212

Chapter Four – The Uncovering	*216*
Chapter Five – All Together Now	*218*
Chapter Six – The Final Part	*219*
Chapter Seven – Good Morning, Harry, Nice Dream?	*221*

Book One

Harry and the Secret Garden

Chapter One – The Voice

'What are you doing Harry?...What are you doing Harry...'

Harry looked around; he was in his back garden on his own, but he kept hearing someone calling out to him. But who could it be? Suddenly, he heard his mummy call him. 'Harry, look after Hugo; he's coming to play with you in the garden. Please...don't let him get dirty, Harry.'

'Yes, Mummy, I will,' said Harry but not very enthusiastically. Hugo came running towards Harry.

'Did you hear someone calling me, Hugo?' asked Harry.

'Yes, Mummy did,' said Hugo straight away.

'No, before that,' replied Harry.

'No, no, I didn't,' said Hugo looking a bit puzzled as to why Harry was asking him.

'I'm sure I heard something,' said Harry as he looked around trying to work out who may have been calling him.

'What are you doing, Harry...What are you doing, Harry?' the mystery voice suddenly called out again!

'See, Hugo,' said Harry triumphantly, 'I told you someone is calling me.'

Hugo nodded; he certainly did hear that, but it was a bit faint, and it seemed to be coming from the other end of the garden. Harry and Hugo went towards the end of the garden. The Alliss Garden was quite big with lots of green stuff in it, which Mrs Alliss called her plants and trees and shrubs. Harry liked his garden because it was big enough to let him run around with his football, play with all his toys, and even ride his bike. It was perfect, he thought to himself.

'I think it's coming from the other side of the gate,' said Hugo.

Now the gate was the entrance to Mr Alliss's part of the garden. It's where he went to grow things called vegetables. Harry and Hugo would get those for their dinner sometimes. Mr Alliss would be very proud of his vegetables and would often say, 'This came from our garden, boys…' The vegetable garden had a high brick wall surrounding it so you couldn't see over it, and the gate was quite big and heavy to open. On it was written in big white writing "Daddy's Secret Garden – Keep out". Mr Alliss didn't like anyone to go into his vegetable garden without him being there; it's a gardener's thing, you see. The boys looked at each other and wondered what to do next. It was at this exact moment that they were both a bit surprised by their friend Isla suddenly calling out to them.

'Harry, Hugo…I'm coming down, wait for me…'

It just so happened that Isla's mummy had come around to see Mrs Alliss and Isla wanted to see the boys in the garden. Now Harry knew that Isla was very clever, so she would know what to do about this mystery voice. Once Isla had arrived by the boys, Harry said, 'I can hear a voice behind this gate, Isla, and it keeps saying, "What are you doing, Harry…What are you doing, Harry?"'

Isla made out that she was listening then said, 'Hmmm, I can't hear anything.'

'I know that, but just wait and listen, you'll hear it,' said Harry, hoping that it will indeed call out again as it had been doing. They waited and waited for what seemed like ages and ages. Isla was by now getting a bit bored and impatient and wanted to do something else, when sure enough they heard the voice saying, '*What are you doing, Harry…What are you doing, Harry?*'

'There you see, I told you so,' said an excited Harry, glad that he had been proved right, 'and it's coming from behind that gate.'

'Okay, let's go in and investigate,' said Isla. Well, if Isla said it was all right to go in, then it was all right to go in. Isla was the clever one, thought Harry to himself. They tried to open the gate, but it was stuck fast. Isla tried first, but it wouldn't budge. Then Hugo tried, but still the gate wouldn't budge. However, when Harry tried, the gate suddenly just swung open very quickly indeed, which took them all by surprise.

Harry went through the gate; he then turned around to speak to Isla and Hugo for them to come through, when it just as suddenly slammed shut in front of them. Isla and Hugo looked at each other. They were a little bit worried as Harry was on the other side of the gate, and try as they might, they couldn't open it.

'Harry,' Isla shouted, 'are you all right?' as she banged on the door for good measure.

'Harry,' Hugo shouted, 'are you all right?' Hugo was now worried that Harry would get into trouble for being in the Secret Garden. But nothing, they didn't hear a murmur from Harry…they were both getting really worried now, thinking if Harry was all right.

'I better get your mummy,' said Isla, and just as she was about to run off to get Mrs Alliss, the gate suddenly swung open again. There stood Harry with a big grin on his face. 'I did shout back,' he said, 'but you must not have heard me.'

'We didn't hear you, Harry,' said Isla, 'honestly, we didn't…' Well, that's another mystery!

Isla and Hugo walked through the gateway, stood by Harry and looked around at the secret garden. Then just as suddenly as it had opened, the big gate just swung shut as it had done for Harry, but they weren't worried, they were all together now.

'Don't worry, Hugo, Harry can always open that gate again,' said Isla with confidence. Harry smiled to himself. *Yes, that gate isn't a problem to me*, he thought, *I can open it anytime I like!* The children continued to look at the vegetable garden. It was quite a big garden, and yes, it did have lots of vegetables planted everywhere. It had little plots which had been dug up and had something different planted in each of them. They were all neatly marked out with a stick at each corner of the plot then tied together with some string. From the string were little bits of silver paper hanging down. None of the children could understand why. Perhaps they might ask, but not right away, as they shouldn't really be in the vegetable garden in the first place! Funnily enough, they had all forgotten about the mystery voice as they had other things on their minds now.

'Let's explore,' said Isla, keen to have a better look around this secret garden.

'Yes,' said Hugo excitedly, well, why not he thought.

'Okay, but carefully,' said Harry, who was a little bit more cautious. Harry knew that this was his daddy's garden, but if they were careful, he was pretty sure his daddy wouldn't mind. At least, he hoped he wouldn't mind! They all went towards what looked like a lot of trees growing at the bottom of the garden. 'I think they are apple trees or something,' said Harry, 'I think Daddy calls it his Orchard.'

'Yes, they are apple trees all right,' agreed Isla. She was the clever one, after all, and knew her apple trees. The children continued going towards the bottom of the garden. This part of the garden hadn't been planted up with vegetables as it was still on M. Alliss's To Do list. That was a list of jobs that needed doing by Mr Alliss, but it was getting longer and longer. Still, that's another story! It was here when they saw what looked like a compost heap. Well, it was a heap of some sorts looking at it from a distance. Harry wasn't sure, as for some reason or other it didn't look quite right to him. So, he went across to explore, with the other two following close behind. They all started to prod and poke the heap with some sticks that they found nearby. There was something solid behind all the dead leaves and old branches that had been piled up in a big heap. They pulled some of the branches away at the bottom of the heap and it was then that they discovered what looked like an old wheel. They continued pulling some of the old branches away and slowly they revealed an old abandoned car that had been left there. It looked to be a very old car with weeds even growing on the roof. It was very dirty and looked a total wreck!

'What is it?' asked Isla. She knew it was a car, but she thought that it looked very interesting, worth investigating to her mind.

'I thought this was going to be a smelly old compost heap, but it looks like we have found an old car that someone has left here to rot away,' said Harry. 'I wonder how it got here though. There's a brick wall surrounding this garden, so how could it have been driven here?' It was a bit of a mystery really, another one to the list!

They walked around the wreck and tried to find a window clean enough so that they could look inside the car. All the car's windows were very dirty, so try as they might to clean the dirt off, they couldn't really see anything inside.

'I think this car is called a Mmm Kkk One, One,' said Hugo. He had found a badge on the old car's boot after he had cleared away some of the leaves and weeds that were covering it and was reading the lettering out.

'What's one of those?' asked Isla.

'I'm not sure, I wonder if it's one of Daddy's old cars, but I don't think so, as he's never mentioned it before. Perhaps we have made a new discovery!' said Harry excitedly. They were now the discoverers!

Now it was true that Mr Alliss did like old cars, and he had a special old car in the garage that he kept very clean and very polished. Mr Alliss was very proud of his old car. It was called an Austin, but that's just about how much Harry knew about it. By now, Hugo and Isla had found the driver's door, so they tried to open it. They pulled as hard as they might, but it was stuck fast.

'We have found the driver's door, Harry, but we can't open it,' called out Isla. 'Can you try it?'

Harry went across to try and open the driver's door, and to his surprise, it just opened with a loud hissing sound. As the door opened, all the old leaves and weeds tumbled down from the car and onto the ground, making it easier to get into the car. There was a light shining inside the car so they could now see the interior.

'How did you do that?' asked a very surprised Isla. 'We both tried the door, but it wouldn't open for us.' Harry just gave one of his little smiles. He wasn't sure why the door just opened for him, but it did!

The children peered inside the car. It was not like any car that they had seen or sat in before. It looked, well, old fashioned I suppose you could say! They then scrambled inside the car. Harry sat in the front seat where the driver usually sits while Hugo and Isla sat in the back. The seats were very comfortable and the car didn't smell nasty or anything like that, in fact, it was very clean inside, which was a big surprise to them. Sitting comfortably inside the car, the driver's door then closed behind them with the same loud hissing sound that Harry had heard the first time he opened it.

'What do all those switches and clocks do, Harry?' Isla asked, pointing to the car's dashboard at the front of the car.

'I'm not really sure,' said Harry, 'but I think that they are all very important.'

'What's that big red button do in the centre of the dash?' asked Isla.

But before Harry could say anything, Hugo shouted out, 'Go on, press it, Harry.' So, Harry did!

Suddenly, everything changed…

They were no longer just sitting in an old car, as they were now wearing spacesuits made from some type of silvery material. All of them had space helmets on as well, but how did any of that possibly happen!

Then from nowhere, the car spoke to them. 'Hello, this is Space Car Ollopa 21 and welcome aboard, please ensure that your seatbelts are fully tightened and prepare for take-off.' The car continued to speak…

'Space Car Ollopa 21 to Mission Control, ready to count down and take off, please confirm.'

The children looked at each other, which was a bit tricky for Harry as he was sitting in the front of the car and had to turn his head with his space helmet on! They were now all sitting there with straps which were a bit like the seatbelts they would put on in their daddy's car, but these were very different. For one thing, they were very tight and went over their shoulders and clipped together in the centre of their bodies. With the belts done up, they could hardly move in their seats. The car's front windscreen no longer looked onto the garden as somehow it was pointing towards a big black sky with twinkling stars in the distance. The car started to shake; there was a loud noise behind them, which then became a roar, and then they heard a voice inside their helmets say, 'Awaiting launch, please confirm…Please confirm…'

Hugo shouted out, 'CONFIRM!' Then they all heard…

'Ten…nine…eight…seven…six…five…four…three…two…one…ignition sequence…All systems green, and we have take off…'

There was a tremendous roar; the car shook violently; it was all a little bit frightening and then it blasted away.

The children were all pinned to their seats by the speed of the take-off. The space car kept going faster and faster and faster. Everything inside the car was shaking including Harry, Isla and Hugo! What was going to happen to them, whose idea was it to press that Red Button! Then after what seemed like an eternity, all that noise magically went away and they appeared to be calmly floating in space. Their little hearts were beating so fast, none of them really understood what had just happened back there. They just looked out of the windows and gazed in wonderment. Hugo was the first to speak. 'What's that big blue thing that's behind us?' he asked.

Isla spoke next. 'Oh, wow, I think that's Earth, that's our planet, Hugo.'

'Are you sure, Isla, isn't that where we all live?' asked Harry.

'Yes, I think so,' said Isla, 'and it looks beautiful, doesn't it?'

'Yes,' said Harry, 'it really, really does.' All the children were filled with wonderment at what they were seeing. Mother Earth. It was so totally beautiful, but strangely, none of the children were frightened any longer. As long as they were all together, they all felt safe. Isla and Hugo knew that Harry would protect them. Harry was just that kind of boy! After a while as they continued travelling in space, the car spoke again.

'Hello, children, this is Space Car Ollopa 21; we are heading towards Planet Smar13. We will arrive in a short while at Space Station 31 as the planned stop. This is where you can have a rest and have something to eat. Are any of you hungry at all?'

'YES…' they all shouted back. Harry was the loudest!

Chapter Two – In the Space Station

Everything seemed to be happening so very fast that soon they were coming close to the space station. It was a very, very big space station, all painted white with a lot of different parts all inter-connected to it. Other spaceships were parked alongside it as well. The number 31 was clearly painted on the side of the central column structure of the space station. It looked so much bigger the closer they got to it.

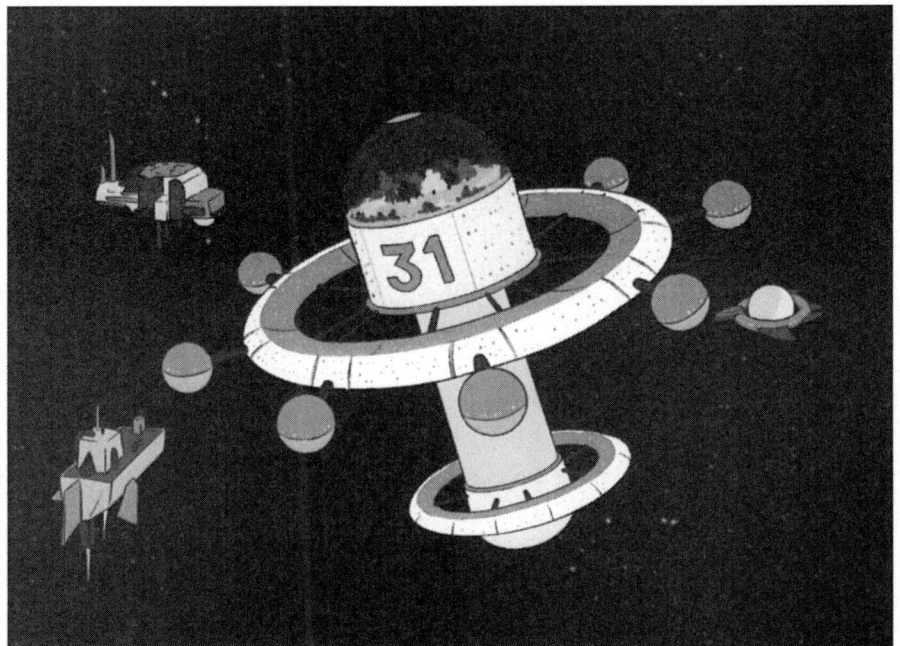

The radio in the space car came on again. 'Hello, Space Car, this is Space Station 31 central control; we have you on radar approach, what is your call sign?'

Harry looked at Isla, Isla looked at Hugo, Hugo looked at Harry. What's a call sign they thought to themselves…

'Mmm Kkk One, One,' Hugo suddenly blurted out.

'Thank you, please proceed to Bay 55, Mmm Kkk One, One.'

'Well done, Hugo!' Harry and Isla gave Hugo a big thumbs up, high praise for thinking that one up.

The space car did as it was instructed and headed towards Bay Number 55. The large outer doors, which were the entrance to the Parking Bay, gently opened to let the space car through and then closed behind them to make it safe to disembark. The space car glided to a stop at Bay Number 55. There were lots of red warning lights appearing on the space car's dashboard, and then one by one they all turned from red to green, with a huge green tick appearing on the front windscreen. The car became very silent and the children didn't dare to speak.

'Welcome to Space Station 31, Bay 55, all systems checked, air lock active, doors now opening,' said the space car.

The doors opened with that same loud hissing sound that the children knew well by now. Harry, Isla and Hugo released their seat straps and got themselves out of the car. There they stood together in complete and total amazement. They had to pinch themselves to make sure it was real, at the same time trying to take in where they had just arrived.

'Welcome to Space Station 31, please proceed to the Rest Area Number 17 where you can relax and order some food,' said a voice from somewhere within the parking bay.

The children took their helmets off and put them down beside the space car. They looked back at the space car they had just arrived in. It was all gleaming in red and looked like it was brand new. It certainly didn't look like the dirty old car they had seen in the secret garden anymore, but it still looked like a car. Harry thought it was funny that it didn't look more like the spaceships they had seen docked by the space station, but no matter it still got them here he thought to himself!

'Which way in the Rest Area Number 17?' asked Hugo.

The children all looked at each other. They didn't know the way to go and the space station looked huge and a little bit overwhelming. Suddenly, a voice came from behind them. 'Hello, I'm Mindy, can I help you?' The children all turned around together, and there was Mindy standing in front of them.

'Don't worry, children, don't be alarmed. I am an AI robot and I've come to help you. AI stands for Artificial Intelligence. I'm from the space station and I have come to take you to Rest Area 17. Please follow me.'

Mindy looked just like a normal girl; she was all dressed in gold, and strangely, she didn't appear to have any feet. Well, as far as the children could see that is, as she just floated slightly above the walkway.

'What's an AI robot, Isla?' asked Hugo.

'It's a very clever robot,' replied Isla.

'Mmm, that's what I thought too,' said Hugo with a cheeky little smile.

Catching up to Mindy and walking alongside her, Hugo asked, 'Mindy, what do you do on this space station?'

'I help fellow travellers like you, to take them to where they need to go. It's very interesting, you meet lots of different people from different galaxies,' said Mindy.

Harry wasn't too sure what all that meant, but Hugo seemed to understand. He continued chatting away with Mindy. In fact, Mindy was now holding Hugo's hand as they went towards the rest area. Well, at least she has hands thought Harry to himself.

Isla looked at Harry and said, 'Isn't this amazing, Harry, I never thought I'd have this much fun today.'

'Nor me,' said Harry; it certainly was a different day to the one he had planned for!

Eventually, they reached the rest area and Mindy showed them to a table.

'What would you like to eat?' asked Mindy.

'Sausages please with chips,' said Harry.

'Cheese and tomato pizza with chips,' said Isla.

'Chocolate ice cream,' said Hugo.

'Very well, coming right up,' said Mindy, 'feel free to share, there will be plenty of food for all three of you. I've added orange squash as well.' And with that, a hatch opened by the side of the table and all the food came out all at once. It really was that quick! Not only that, the food smelled amazing, and as it turned out, it tasted even better.

'That's the best food I have ever had,' said Harry when they finished their meal. Hugo and Isla nodded in agreement, they thought so too.

Chapter Three – Homeward Bound

'Oi, kids, what are you up to; where are you going; come over here I want to talk to you.'

They all turned around and saw what they first thought was another robot, but it looked very scruffily dressed for a robot. It wasn't a robot at all but another space traveller who said that his name was Martian, and he needed a lift to Planet 99Ekalfa.

Harry wasn't too sure if this Martian was friendly or not. He seemed very rough and had a nasty looking face, with a crooked nose and dirty unkempt hair. Harry was a bit wary of him. However, before he even said another word, Mindy re-appeared and told the space traveller that they weren't going anywhere near Planet 99Ekalfa and so not to bother them.

'Okay, okay,' said Martian, 'keep your microchip on,' and walked away in a huff.

'Good luck with your trip, kids,' he said with a smirk which Harry certainly didn't like.

'Thank you, Mindy,' said Harry. 'I really didn't like that space traveller; he gave me the shivers!'

'Oh, don't worry, we get all types here at Space Station 31, that's why I came back to make sure that you were all right. Usually, these space travellers appear to be worse than their bite, but you must remember that they all come from different galaxies and so have different ways how they talk and interact with each other. But you are right to be wary of that one. I don't like him much myself. He's been here for ages, nobody wants to give him a lift; it's not a planet anyone wants to visit,' admitted Mindy.

'Thank you, Mindy, for looking after us,' said Hugo. 'I think you're really lovely.'

'Ahh, thank you, Hugo,' said Mindy, 'that's so kind of you, but it's my job!'

Isla looked at Harry and Harry looked at Isla and they both looked as Mindy and Hugo were walking back together to the space car holding hands. It was that kind of day thought Harry to himself, just full of surprises. It's going to be difficult to explain it all to his mummy when they get back!

When they eventually got back to the space car in Bay 55, Harry thanked Mindy, 'Thank you for looking after us, Mindy; we're very sad to have to go, but I think our parents might be getting worried about us; we have been gone a long time now.'

'That's all right,' said Mindy, 'I understand, I was very happy you meet you and look after you.'

'Thank you, Mindy!' they all shouted together.

The children made to put their space helmets back on and got back into the space car. The doors opened and closed with that same loud hiss as before. Once they had strapped themselves in, they waved to Mindy as she made her way back to the safety of the Parking Bay viewing area. Harry now thought to himself how he was going to get the space car to take them back home.

He didn't really understand any of the controls, so crossing his fingers on both hands, he spoke to Isla and Hugo. 'I better tell this car that we need to go home now; I really hope it understands me…Hello, Ollopa 21, can you take us home now please to Planet Earth and land back in my daddy's Secret Garden?' asked Harry.

There was a few moments silence and Harry's heart beat ever faster and faster. Will the car understand, can they leave the space station or will they be stuck here like Martian? It was a nervous moment for all the children…

Then the space car spoke. 'Yes, understand command, will execute…Altering course coordinates to Planet Earth…Re-computing…Please wait…Checking all systems…Please ensure you are all strapped in…Getting confirmation from Space Station Control…Please wait…Starting take-off sequence…All systems now checked…We are green to go…Outer Bay doors are opening…Commencing ignition sequence…'

Harry breathed a sigh of relief; the car was doing exactly as it was told; what a good space car this is thought Harry! This time, the space car didn't make a lot of noise; it just moved forward very gently heading towards the outer doors of the space station docking area. Then once clear of the doors, the children heard a tremendous roaring noise. The same noise that they had heard when the space car had blasted off from the Secret Garden. The car shook a lot this time as it accelerated and then whoosh they were gone. The children were all pinned to their seats as the car kept accelerating forward going ever faster and faster. It was very scary but awesome all at the same time; it was all a blur! Eventually, the car reached its top speed and everything went quiet again and the shaking stopped.

'Hello, this is Space Car Ollopa 21; we have reached maximum cruising speed, next destination is Planet Earth. Please enjoy the flight. Out.'

'Phew, I'm glad that's over,' said Harry, 'this space travelling isn't as easy as I thought.'

'Hugo has gone a bit green, Harry, but I think he's all right now,' said Isla looking at poor Hugo who really didn't enjoy that take-off. Perhaps it was all that ice cream he ate in the space station! After a while travelling through space, the children eventually spotted a planet in front of them. 'What's that big blue thing in front of us?' asked Hugo.

'You should know that by now, Hugo, that's home,' said Isla with a big sigh but ever so happy to see Earth again. All the children now thought of Earth as their home.

'Yes, that's our Planet Earth, Hugo, our home, and it's just so beautiful, welcome home, everybody,' said Harry; he was overjoyed; it really had been one amazing day.

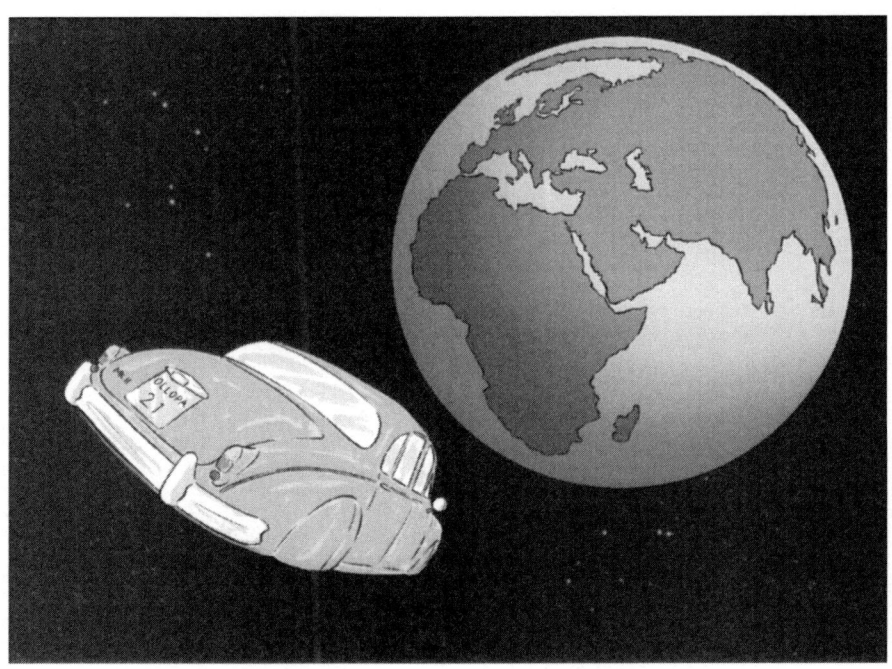

Over the space car's radio boomed an announcement, 'Lowering heat shields, approaching Earth's atmosphere, please ensure you are strapped in; it will get very noisy, no further communications, out.' And everything went quiet again ready for re-entry…they were almost home!

Chapter Four – The Explanation

The next thing they all knew was that the space car had landed back in Daddy's Secret Garden. They all got out of the car and walked back towards the garden gate. Somehow they were all normally dressed again, but where had their space suits all gone? How did they get changed back into their normal clothes? Harry didn't remember any of them changing inside the space car; there's no room inside the car to do that in any case. Now that was another mystery to add to the list!

Harry looked back one more time to where the space car was parked and was a bit surprised by what he saw. The space car looked exactly as they found it before their space adventure. It had become the same old compost heap they found, almost all of it was now covered in leaves and weeds and it had branches all over the top of it. What bits of it he could still see looked all dirty and you couldn't see through any of the windows anymore. *How did that happen*, thought Harry to himself, *we didn't put the branches back on the car?*

'Come on, Harry,' shouted Isla,' our parents will be wondering where we have got to.' *Yes*, Harry thought to himself, *we have been gone for ages and ages, this might be difficult to explain!* It was at that moment that Harry looked down by the garden gate, and there in the soil lay a mobile phone. It was a bit dirty, but he picked it up and put it in his pocket. Then as he went through the gate, it just slammed shut behind him.

'Mummy, Mummy, Mummy!' they all shouted as they ran up the garden and into the house. Mrs Alliss and Isla's mummy were both sitting in the kitchen having a cup of tea and looked around a bit startled as the children ran in.

'Oh my,' said Mrs Alliss, 'you're all back very early; didn't you find anything to do in the garden?'

That caught the children by surprise and they went very quiet. Harry couldn't understand what his mummy had just said, because he thought that they had been gone for a very long time. Then he remembered that he had picked up that old mobile phone on his way out of the Secret Garden and had put it in his back pocket, so he took it out to have a look.

'Oh my, that's my mobile phone!' called out Mr Alliss who had just walked into the kitchen. 'Where on earth did you find it, Harry? I've been trying to find it this morning; I must have mislaid it by accident. Gosh, it's a bit mucky, but never mind, it's got a new ringtone let me show you, Harry.' And Mr Alliss played his new ringtone… 'Harry, what are you doing? Harry, what are you doing…'?

'Neat, eh, Harry, don't you think?' said Mr Alliss.

'Yes, very neat, Daddy,' said Harry, not really knowing what else to say. He was still in shock with what his mummy had first said when they came into the kitchen.

'Well, that's made my day, Harry,' said Mr Alliss. So that was the mystery of the voice that Harry had heard. It was his daddy's mobile phone with its new ringtone! Well, at least one mystery had been solved today thought Harry.

'Where did you find it, Harry?' asked Mr Alliss.

But before Harry could answer, Isla said, 'Oh, we found it in the grass by the gate to your Secret Garden.' She gave Harry a knowing wink and he smiled back. *That's good thinking, Isla,* thought Harry.

'Oh,' said Mr Alliss, 'that's okay then, probably the reason why it's so mucky it's been laying on the grass, but thank you very much; I thought I might have lost it.'

'Can we go and watch some TV now, Daddy, we're all a little bit tired,' asked Harry.

'Well, normally it would be a no, but in this instance, it's a yes, as a reward for finding my phone, but I'm surprised that you're all tired, children, you've only been playing for a short while,' said Mr Alliss.

Chapter Five – Did It Ever Happen?

Harry, Isla and Hugo went it into the front room, closed the door behind them, put the TV on and sat on the sofa. They all looked at each other; they were now all a bit unsure as to what really had happened today. Did it happen or was it just a dream or something else?

Isla was the first to speak; she turned around to both boys and said, 'Did that really happen, Harry? I mean the space station and the space car and the space trip. It was all amazing, but did it really happen? Your mummy and daddy said we were only gone for few minutes, but how could that be? It felt like we were gone for ages and ages. It couldn't have happened, Harry, it just couldn't; it must have been a dream or something.'

Harry didn't say anything straight away, because to him it also seemed very real as well, but he couldn't explain it either. Especially after his daddy and mummy said they were only gone for a short while, that really confused him as well!

'When Mummy said we were only gone a few minutes, I was a bit surprised as well. No, very surprised,' Harry said eventually, 'but it seemed very real to me. When we got back and before I went through the gate, I looked back at the space car and it was just an old compost heap like the one we found. I really don't understand it at all.'

Then Hugo stood up and took what looked like a badge out of his pocket and passed it to Harry and Isla to look at.

'Mindy gave me that; it's her badge,' said Hugo.

Harry looked at it. It was bright silver, heavy and had some writing on it, it said...

Mindy – Space Station 31

Always Happy to Help

Call 81-81-81

They all looked at it and then all broke out with huge smiles.

'That really was the best adventure ever…' they all said together. 😊

Harry and the Ill Little Girl

Chapter One – Going to Hospital

It was a cold and frosty Saturday morning when Harry woke up. He looked out of his bedroom window. No snow he thought to himself. *What a pity, I would like to have built a snowman with my brother*, Harry mused to himself. He then got dressed, went into the bathroom, brushed his teeth and combed his hair, and with that, he went downstairs to see his mummy.

'What's for breakfast, Mummy?' asked Harry.

'Oh, Harry, I haven't got much time this morning, your brother and daddy had to dash out to get Hugo's new football kit, so it's just the two of us this morning, and I have got a hospital appointment this morning, Harry. Can you quickly eat some cereal as we need to leave very soon?' asked Mrs Alliss. So, Harry did as he was told; he got out this favourite cereal and some cold milk and ate it as quickly as he could.

'I've finished, Mummy,' said Harry.

'Well done, Harry, thank you for being so quick. Now put on your coat and shoes as we must go,' said Mrs Alliss. They both left the house and walked down the road to the bus stop. Harry knew that the family car had been taken by his daddy so it wasn't worth asking about a lift to the hospital. They waited and waited in the cold for some time as there were some roadworks which were delaying the bus service. Eventually, a big red bus appeared and Harry and his mummy boarded the bus. Why is it that buses always have this funny smell thought Harry to himself, but at least, they could sit together as there was a pair of seats unoccupied? The hospital wasn't too far away and they soon got there, but it did give Harry a bit of time to warm up as it was a very cold day. The bus stopped right outside the hospital and they both walked into the hospital's entrance hall.

'I have an appointment with Doctor Angela Withstanley,' said Mrs Alliss to the receptionist. The receptionist looked at them both and then checked her computer screen for the appointment.

'Yes, I see it, Doctor Withstanley is running a bit late, I'm afraid,' said the receptionist.

'Oh, how late?' enquired Mrs Alliss.

'Oh, about 20 minutes or so,' she replied.

Harry rolled his eyes; he could have had some toast with jam as well and perhaps a cup of tea had he known that he would have to wait even longer now. The receptionist caught sight of Harry making a face and explained, 'Doctor Withstanley had an emergency to attend to earlier on, that's why she's late.'

That made Harry feel really bad; he didn't want to seem un-caring. He slumped his shoulders and felt a little bit silly. His mummy ruffled his hair and said, 'Don't worry, Harry, we weren't to know.' And even the receptionist broke into a smile! They sat in the reception hall when eventually Dr Withstanley's secretary came down to collect them.

'I'm sorry, Doctor Withstanley was running a bit late this morning, but she's ready now, please come upstairs and you can wait in Doctor Withstanley's surgery. It's not so noisy as down here and you can have a cup of tea or coffee if you like.' They followed the secretary to Doctor Withstanley's surgery and took a seat. Harry sat down next to a little girl who was also sitting there.

Within a few minutes, a voice called out, 'Mrs Alliss, Doctor Withstanley will see you now, Room 2 please.'

'Now, Harry, you stay here and I won't be too long,' said Mrs Alliss as she got up to go and see her doctor.

Chapter Two – Meeting Ellie and Lady Vix

'Are you seeing the doctor as well?' asked the little girl sitting next to Harry.

'No,' replied Harry, 'it's just my mummy; I'm not seeing the doctor.'

'Oh, I am, I have had an appointment; I may have to go into hospital,' said the little girl. Harry never thought that young children like him needed to go to hospital; he just thought hospitals were only for grownups.

'Why?' asked Harry.

'I'm not feeling very well. I'm always tired; I can't breathe very well and I have a headache as well nearly all the time,' the little girl replied.

'Where's your mummy?' asked Harry.

'She's with the doctor, talking about me and stuff, why do grownups do that?'

Harry nodded. 'Yes, why can't we talk to the doctor as well,' he said.

'I think it's so unfair,' said the little girl.

'What's your name?' Harry asked.

'Ellie.'

'Mine's Harry.'

'Do you like playing football?' continued Harry; he thought that at least he could have a chat with Ellie while he waited for his mummy to finish her appointment, and football was one of his favourite topics!

'No,' was the very short reply.

'What do you like then?' asked Harry, realising that he was now getting a bit short of things to talk about now that Ellie didn't like football!

'I like playing with my dolls,' said Ellie.

Oh no, Harry thought that was so boring, but he didn't want to say so, as he didn't want to appear to be rude.

'I do like reading adventure stories as well,' said Ellie.

'Do you? I just love adventure stories as well,' replied Harry enthusiastically. 'My Aunty Dare tells me lots of adventure stories; she tells really good stories.' But before they started to talk a little bit more about these stories, the main door to the surgery opened and a tall very well-dressed lady walked in. Surprisingly, she came over to where Harry and Ellie were both sitting and they both looked up. The children looked at the lady as she stood there before them. She was beautifully dressed, and Harry thought that her perfume was very nice.

'Hello, you two, I'm Lady Vix. Aunty Dare told me that you may be here so I thought I would come over and say hello to you, Harry.' Harry's face brightened up; he loved his Aunty Dare and thought Lady Vix was very nice as well, but Ellie wasn't too sure who this lady could possibly be. Lady Vix could see that Ellie looked a bit flustered and unsure with her. 'Don't worry, I won't bite you, young lady,' said Lady Vix looking at Ellie.

'No, miss,' said Ellie still feeling quite unsure as to who this person was.

'Now you said that you like adventure, Ellie, so have you noticed anything?' asked Lady Vix. Now how did she know that, thought Harry; he only knew about that a few minutes ago when Ellie told him!

No, I don't notice anything different at all,' said Ellie, not really getting where all this was leading to. Even Harry looked around him as well. Everything seemed pretty normal to him as well.

'Take your time, Ellie,' said Lady Vix. Ellie really didn't understand what was it that may have changed around her. She didn't reply for a few minutes but kept looking up at Lady Vix who stood there with a nice smile on her face.

Then after a few minutes, Ellie responded, 'Well, no, actually I'm starting to feel a little bit better,' she said with a smile. 'I can breathe more easily and don't have a headache anymore, but that's not normal for me to feel like that!'

'Good, there you are, child, you have noticed something new; it could very well be the start of a new adventure for you!' said Lady Vix. Then turning to the surgery's receptionist, Lady Vix said in a loud voice. 'We're going to the restaurant downstairs to catch some breakfast, call me on my mobile when I'm required. These two children will be joining me. Do you understand…?'

'Oh, yes, Lady Vix,' said the receptionist almost getting up onto her feet when she replied. She really understood everything that Lady Vix said when she was in full voice.

'Okay, you two, let's be quick, the food won't stay warm forever. You are hungry I take it?' enquired Lady Vix.

'Oh, yes,' they both replied, and the three of then went out of the waiting room, with Lady Vix out in front walking at a very brisk pace and with Ellie and Harry almost having to run close behind just to keep up with her.

'I'm not walking too fast for you, am I?' asked Lady Vix looking at her charge as they were somewhat lagging behind her.

'No, no, we're fine,' said Harry, looking at Ellie hoping that she was also fine.

'Yes, I'm fine as well. I couldn't run at all this morning, but I'm feeling so much better now,' said Ellie.

'Good, excellent, I knew you would be…now come along, children, let's not dawdle otherwise all the food will be gone.'

Chapter Three – The Breakfast

They all arrived at the restaurant and Lady Vix went straight to the front of the queue. When a man who was standing there ready to be served looked at Lady Vix, she just stared right back at him. Harry knew that look; his mummy could throw that look sometimes. It could freeze water at ten steps. The man dropped his stare, began looking a little bit sheepish and then said, 'No, please, after you, Your Ladyship.'

'Thank you,' said Lady Vix. Gosh, Harry thought to himself, sometimes his mummy could be mighty but Lady Vix was something else!

Looking at the lady serving behind the counter, Lady Vix said, 'Can we have my normal breakfast please, but for three. These children will have smaller portions please. We haven't got long so be quick about it…Thank you.' The waitress who took the order simply said "Yes" and then didn't say another word. Lady Vix waved her credit card, pressed some buttons on the card machine that the lady behind the counter offered and then made her way to sit down at a table. Gosh, thought Harry, he's never seen anything like this before. Lady Vix was right, it certainly is a new adventure!

Breakfast arrived very quickly, which surprised both children. It was all piping hot and there was a lot of it as well. Porridge, smoked salmon, eggs boiled, scrambled and fried, bacon, sausages, toast and a pot of tea. Goodness, there was so much food!

'Let's eat, children, no time to be lost today. I have got a lot to do today, tuck in,' said Lady Vix.

Well, even though there was so much food on the table somehow, to both children's surprise, it was all eaten up. Everything, right down to the toast and marmalade. It was all scrumptious!

'I always think a good breakfast is essential to set you up for the day,' said Lady Vix, 'don't you agree, children?'

'Yes,' they both said together, nodding their heads with big smiles on their faces. Harry and Ellie both leaned back on their chairs, their bellies were fit to burst. How did they manage to eat so much food, thought Harry, but somehow they did, and Ellie really tucked in with gusto!

'Very good, let's go back now as I feel that my phone will be going off any minute now,' said Lady Vix. They all got up and made their way back to the surgery waiting room.

'Thank you for the breakfast, Lady Vix, it was delicious; it was the best breakfast ever,' said Harry.

'Yes, thank you very much, Lady Vix,' said Ellie. 'I've never eaten so much! I agree with Harry, that was the best breakfast I've ever had.'

'You're more than welcome, now, children, let's be on our way,' said Lady Vix. When they got back to the surgery waiting room, the children went back to their seats and Lady Vix went straight into a room to see her doctor.

'I bet the doctor is pretty scared of Lady Vix,' said Harry to Ellie, 'you really don't mess with her!'

'Oh, I think she really nice; she's made me feel so much better,' said Ellie who was now feeling so much better than she did when she first came to the hospital this morning. Just then Harry's mummy came up to them having finished her appointment with her doctor. 'Ready to go, Harry?'

'Yes, Mummy, ready. Bye, Ellie, hope to see you again,' said Harry.

'Bye, Harry, it was great fun today,' said Ellie, and with that, Harry went off with his mummy.

'I see that you had a nice little chat with that little girl,' said Mrs Alliss.

'Yes, she's quite nice really. We went down for breakfast with Lady Vix,' said Harry.

'And whose is Lady Vix?' asked Mrs Alliss with a quizzical tone, certainly a new name that she hadn't heard of before.

'Oh, er, she's Aunty Dare's friend,' said Harry a bit sheepishly, wondering if he had done something wrong.

'Oh, Aunty Dare…well, she does know a lot of people, doesn't she, Harry, and you had breakfast as well? What sort of breakfast Harry?' continued Mrs Alliss.

'We had porridge and salmon and eggs and sausages and bacon…'

'Stop…!' said Mrs Alliss. 'You can't get a dried ham sandwich in that restaurant, Harry, just tell me the truth.'

'We did, Mummy, we did…honestly,' said Harry.

'Mmm,' said Mrs Alliss, 'not one of your little adventures, is it, Harry?' Harry thought it best not to say anymore; it was becoming a bit difficult to explain.

'Do you have to go back to see the doctor again, Mummy?' asked Harry wisely changing the subject.

'Yes, in two weeks' time. I'll look forward to meeting Lady Vix then…that is if she ever appears!' said Mrs Alliss quite sternly.

Chapter Four – The Return Visit

Two weeks went by and Harry was again going back to the hospital with his mummy, as his brother was playing a school football match and needed a lift, and Mr Alliss had to take some of Hugo's teammates in the family car as well to the match. So, it was just the two of them.

Harry was a little bit nervous in case Ellie's mother was going to be there. He really didn't know what to expect. They walked into the surgery and there sitting in the waiting room was Ellie. She looked completely different from the last time Harry saw her. She was swinging her legs to and fro on her chair, had a big smile on her face and was looking very happy with herself indeed. She gave Harry a big wave when she saw him. 'Hello, Harry!' she shouted across the reception area waiting room. Everyone looked around.

Harry and Mrs Alliss sat down close to where Ellie was sitting and a woman who Harry had never seen before came up to him and asked, 'Are you Harry?'

'Err, yes, I think so,' said Harry feeling a little bit worried and tucking himself slightly behind his mummy as this woman was looking directly at him.

'What did you do to my daughter?' she asked in a slightly pointed manner.

'Nothing, nothing, nothing,' Harry kept saying, feeling a little bit worried what this lady was going to do or say next.

Looking at Mrs Alliss, the woman then said, 'Are you Harry's mother, do you know what happened the last time you were both here?'

'Yes, I am, but I don't know exactly what happened, but I did hear about a Lady Vix and some breakfast they may have had together. Is there any problem here?' Mrs Alliss enquired. She felt very defensive towards Harry, but she didn't quite know what had happened here either.

'Yes, I would really like to meet her. Look at my daughter, she's changed. I mean completely changed but for the better! I mean she's now completely and utterly well. She's so happy, and it's just so incredible,' Ellie's mother continued, but now she was beaming and her voice was getting more and more excited. 'I really don't know what happened here, but thank you, Harry, thank you,' she said. 'I want to give you a big hug, Harry.' Harry shrunk back in his seat; he really wasn't sure whether this lady was happy with him or not.

'GO LADY VIX…' Ellie shouted at the top of her voice. Everyone in the waiting room looked around, even the doctors came out of their rooms to see what was happening. Just at that moment, the main door to the surgery opened and a tall elegant lady walked in.

'Hello, Lady Vix,' Harry said, just so relieved that she had arrived. Perhaps she will now explain everything and take the attention away from him Harry thought.

'Hello, Harry, have you had breakfast yet…'

Lady Vix didn't wait for a reply. 'No, well, no matter we can go downstairs and have some. You can take your friend as well if you like.' Turning to Mrs Alliss and Ellie's mummy, Lady Vix said, 'We won't be long, dears.' And with that, she turned around and walked towards the restaurant. Harry and Ellie followed; it seemed the right thing to do thought Harry. Mrs Alliss and Ellie's mummy just looked at each other with their mouths wide open not really knowing what to say as the threesome went down to have breakfast together.

Chapter Five – What to Do?

Mrs Alliss and Mrs Sage-Browne, Ellie's mummy, sat down beside each other in the reception area after Harry, Ellie and Lady Vix had left the room and started to have a chat together.

'You can't get as much as an egg sandwich in that restaurant, and that's on a good day,' said Mrs Alliss with an air of total disbelief.

'I know, I know, but Ellie told me about this feast that she had,' said Mrs Sage-Browne, 'but my daughter isn't a fibber.'

'Nor my Harry,' said Mrs Alliss.

'Well, they're going down now, shall we follow them?' said Mrs Sage-Browne.

'I'm in two minds, but I don't want to miss my appointment with my doctor,' said Mrs Alliss trying to think of a good reason why she shouldn't go.

'Yes, nor me,' said Mrs Sage-Browne, 'it's a bother really as I would like to see this feast, I must admit.' Both mothers were now in a bit of a bind. Do they go down or do they not go down to the restaurant? What to do?

'The thing is your daughter Ellie is now so much better, so that's got to be a good thing. Perhaps we should leave them alone as I don't want to be doubting my Harry,' said Mrs Alliss.

'Yes, I agree, it would make us look bad as it has all ended up so well for my Ellie,' said Mrs Sage-Browne.

'What did the doctor say about Ellie, after her sudden improvement?' asked Mrs Alliss with great interest.

'He was totally mystified about it all but explained it by saying the human body is an amazing machine and can sometimes fix itself. Not much of an explanation I must admit, but it will have to do for now,' said Mrs Sage-Browne.

'Who is Lady Vix?' enquired Mrs Sage-Browne.

'Hmmm, I don't really know. She appears to be a friend of Harry's favourite aunty…Aunty Dare. I have a feeling that Lady Vix will be very much part of my Harry's adventures from now on…'

Harry, Aunty Dare and Her Magical Motor Scooter

Chapter One – Aunty Dare

Harry was sitting in the front room, and well, he was bored, very bored in fact. His bother Hugo had gone to play football with his daddy and they had left Harry at home. Harry had a bit of a cold and a bit of a cough and he was told he had to stay indoors. He had read all his books and didn't want to watch anymore television either. He was told that he couldn't play with his friends. What was there left to do! He could hear his mummy working in the kitchen, but she told him that he couldn't help her as she didn't want him coughing on the food and spreading any of his germs. What to do he thought…

Suddenly, he heard the distinctive pop, pop, pop sound of a motor scooter coming up the driveway. Harry rushed to the front room window, and there he could see Aunty Dare arriving on her motor scooter. He waved excitedly to Aunty Dare and she waved back. Aunty Dare was always great fun to be with and had lots of stories to tell Harry and she always managed to do exciting things. Aunty Dare was Harry's favourite aunty; she was very important to him. She always had a big smile and a happy way about her.

This really cheered Harry up. She also always had some chocolate with her that she shared with Harry, even when his mummy wasn't looking. Aunty Dare rang the doorbell and Harry rushed to open the front door, but his mummy was there already and stopped him.

'I'll open the front door, Harry, you go back to the front room please,' said Mrs Alliss. Harry's excitement evaporated. He now thought that his mummy would tell Aunty Dare that she couldn't come in and let her see him. Harry sloped back to the front room, feeling so very disappointed.

'Oh, Hello, Aunty Dare,' said Mrs Alliss. 'Harry is not very well today so he's not allowed to go anywhere.

'Oh, that's all right, Nicola,' replied Aunty Dare in her cheery way. 'I've come to see you. I'll just pop my head around to say hello to Harry. I'll keep my distance, I promise.'

Mrs Alliss was wrong footed; she felt that she had to let Harry see his Aunty Dare now. She couldn't be that mean to him, so she let Aunty Dare into the house. 'Okay, I'll be in the kitchen, and if you like, I'll make you a cup of tea,' said Mrs Alliss and went back into her kitchen.

Aunty Dare waited till Mrs Alliss closed the door to the kitchen and then went into the front room. Harry immediately ran up to her, and although he wasn't supposed to, he gave her a big, big, super squeeze. Aunty Dare didn't mind at all!

'Lovely to see you, Harry,' said Aunty Dare giving Harry a big hug as well.

'Lovely to see you, Aunty,' replied Harry excitedly. 'I've got a cold so I been told by Mummy that I can't go anywhere…but I'm so bored, Aunty!'

'Yes, your mummy told me that, but don't worry, Harry, we can still go out together.'

'Oh, I don't think Mummy will let us, Aunty, she's very strict with me,' said Harry disappointedly.

Aunty Dare had that mischievous look on her face that Harry knew and loved so much. 'Oh, don't worry she won't know we're even gone, Harry.' And she gave Harry a knowing wink.

'But she's got really good hearing you know, Aunty. She always knows what I'm doing and that's so annoying sometimes,' said Harry. He went back and slumped in his armchair and Aunty Dare sat on the opposite armchair in the front room.

'What we'll do is stay here in the front room but also go out at all at the same time,' said Aunty Dare. Now Harry had never heard of such a thing before, so to say the least he was a little bit puzzled.

'How do we do that, Aunty?' asked Harry with a perplexed look.

'Oh, it's all down to the Laws of Bilocation and time control; it's all very simple once you know what you're doing…now, Harry, listen carefully,' said Aunty Dare. She got out of her armchair and stood by the door, but now suddenly, there were two Aunty Dares. One sitting and one standing. Harry couldn't quite believe what he was seeing.

'Ggggggosh,' Harry said, 'that's mmmmmagic, Aunty!'

'Okay, Harry, now you come towards me.' So, Harry got up and walked across to Aunty Dare who was standing by the door. 'Now look behind you,' said Aunty Dare, and sure enough, there were now two Harrys. One standing by Aunty Dare and one sitting in the armchair. 'Right, we'll now let Aunty Dare number 2 and Harry number 2 chat away together and we'll both go out,' said Aunty Dare, the real one that is!

Harry walked up to his magical double and listened. He could hear what appeared to be himself talking to Aunty Dare, but he really couldn't understand what they were both saying to each other. 'Oh, it's just idle chit chat, it's not supposed to make any sense,' said Aunty Dare, 'so that if your mummy pops her head around, she'll think everything's fine, should she look in of course.'

'But I'm sure she will see us go out of the house though,' said Harry. Aunty Dare took Harry's hand and went to go out through the kitchen. Harry really wasn't too sure about that, surely, they'll be seen by his mummy! There was Mrs Alliss preparing food for this evening's dinner. She was peeling potatoes, making a chocolate brownie cake, Harry's favourite, and getting ready to sit down with a fresh cup of tea.

Harry just froze. 'She can see us, Aunty Dare, she can she see us…' he whispered.

But Aunty Dare just went right up to Harry's mummy and waved her hand right in front of her face. Nothing, not a sausage, no reaction…Mrs Alliss didn't give any sign that Aunty Dare was right there standing in front of her! 'See, Harry, we are invisible now,' said Aunty Dare.

Aunty Dare then made to go through the kitchen door, but instead of opening it, she just walked straight through it. Well, Harry couldn't believe what he just saw. After a few moments, Aunty Dare popped her head literally through the kitchen door and said, 'Come on, Harry, no time to waste.'

Harry inched slowly forward with his arm out expecting it to hit on the solid kitchen door, but no…his arm went straight through the door, and in the next second, there he was standing outside in the garden with his aunty. Harry was totally amazed by what just happened, but then magic always happens when he's with his Aunty Dare, and she rarely disappoints!

Chapter Two – The Magical Tour

In the back garden, there stood Aunty Dare's motor scooter. It was all gleaming in a lovely metallic brown colour that made it look very swish. Some people said it was more orange, but Harry felt sure it was brown. 'I thought you had left your motor scooter outside the front door, Aunty,' said Harry, again a little bit puzzled.

'Yes, Harry, you're right I did, but remember, there are now two of us and so two motor scooters as well,' explained Aunty Dare. It was all very confusing to Harry, but it slowly was making sense, well, at least some bits of it were…

Aunty Dare handed Harry a crash helmet and then got on to start the scooter up. 'Put the helmet on, Harry, and hop on…Hold tight now.' And off they both went.

Well, traffic isn't a problem when you ride a magic motor scooter, as it just goes right through everything in the road. Cars, buses, lorries, vans…well, just everything! The magic scooter made light work of all the traffic, and they eventually arrived at Buckingham Palace and parked on the mall which is the big pink road that leads up to the palace.

'Off you pop, Harry, I've just got one more thing to do before we start to explore,' said Aunty Dare. Harry got off the scooter, and with that, Aunty Dare raised the scooter's seat to reveal a cubby hole from which she pulled out what looked to Harry to be a large mobile phone with a pole attached to it. This extended above the scooter and then started to spin around and around making a funny sound like a deep hum. Aunty Dare turned a switch on the scooter's handlebar. Then the magic started.

Everything just stopped, and I mean everything! All the traffic, the cars, the buses, the taxis, the vans, the lorries and even the people, they just all stopped in their tracks. They didn't move at all!

'Wow, Aunty, how did you do that?' asked a very wide-eyed and very amazed Harry.

'I just slowed everything right down, Harry, using my reverse vectoring transmitter quadrant. I thought I'd test it out today, as you never know when you might need it, Harry. So, now we are travelling very fast, but everyone else is travelling very, very, very slowly. I can't stop time, I'm not that clever, but I can make it appear that I have slowed it down a bit,' said Aunty Dare. 'When we get back, everything will have moved a little bit, Harry.'

'How much is a little bit, Aunty?' asked Harry.

'Oh, about this much.' And Aunty Dare put her thumb and finger together leaving just a tiny, tiny little gap.

'Gosh,' said Harry; it seemed the only thing left to say; it was all so totally magical, fantastical and completely out of this world, which of course it was!

'Let's go into the palace, Harry and see the queen. I would like to have tea with the queen,' said Aunty Dare. 'Oh no, wait! The Royal Standard is not flying today, that means the queen isn't in. What a shame, I would have liked to have seen the queen today,' said Aunty Dare. 'I guess it will have to wait for another time.' Aunty Dare thought for a few seconds then said, 'I know let's go to Downing Street where the prime minister of Britain lives; I haven't been there before, have you, Harry?' Harry just shook his head; words were completely failing him now.

So, they both got back on the motor scooter and rode the short distance to Downing Street, which in case you didn't know isn't very far away from Buckingham Palace, and then parked up outside the big black door of Number 10, Downing Street.

'Oh, good, the prime minister is in, let's go and see him,' said Aunty Dare.

Harry saluted the policeman who stood like a statue outside the big black front door. They then went right through the big black door and once inside turned down the corridor to the big room where there was a long table with lots of chairs around it. In the room, they could see two men. One was sitting in a big chair in the middle of the long table and was pointing a finger at another man who was standing on the opposite side of the table. He had a rather long face like he had eaten something that wasn't very nice, like a lemon perhaps.

'Looks like our prime minister is giving someone a telling off,' said Aunty Dare.

'How can you tell, Aunty?' asked Harry.

'Oh, it's a look that I'm used to seeing, Harry, trust me, I'm your aunty.' It was at this point that Harry felt his tummy rumble.

'I'm a bit hungry, Aunty, can we eat something?' said Harry. Harry always got hungry when he was doing exciting things. It was all that nervous energy he was using up his aunty would say to him.

'Well, no, Harry, sorry about that, but when we are using the reverse vectoring transmitter quadrant, it won't allow us to eat anything. I'm sorry, but that's the law of time and physics,' said Aunty Dare. Well, Harry wasn't going to argue with any of that, I mean, who would? He didn't understand a single word of what Aunty Dare had said except the no bit; he understood that all right!

'Okay, Aunty, I understand, we must obey the law,' said Harry; it seemed the right thing to say. Aunty Dare gave Harry a big smile and ruffled his hair.

'Well done, Harry, you'll be a science professor very soon.'

'I'm still hungry though,' said Harry. Then Aunty Dare remembered that she had brought some chocolate. She reached inside her leather rider's jacket pocket and brought out a bar of chocolate. Harrys eyes went wide open.

'I thought that we couldn't eat anything, Aunty?' said Harry.

'Yes, you are absolutely right, Harry, but it's not a problem providing I brought it with me when the vectoring transmitter did the computation as it reenergises the chocolate for eating.' *Gosh*, thought Harry, *my aunty is so clever*. He didn't really understand anything except the eating bit; Harry understood that part all right. Breaking the chocolate bar into half, they both ate each chocolate cube very slowly, allowing the lovely smooth tasty chocolate to dissolve in their mouths…it tasted so delicious.

'Mummy doesn't like me to eat too much chocolate, Aunty,' said Harry. 'She tells me off if I have too much.'

'Oh, don't worry, Harry, I won't grass you up,' said Aunty Dare with that ever so naughty wink of hers.

Harry just smiled; it was so much fun being with Aunty Dare; she wasn't like any of the other aunties he knew. 'Right, Harry, we'll go around London and see the sights. Trafalgar Square, Houses of Parliament, HMS Belfast, the Tower of London, is that all right with you, Harry?'

'Oh, yes, please that sounds fantastic,' said Harry. So, they left No. 10 Downing Street and got back on the magical motor scooter and zoomed off. Aunty Dare chose to put the scooter into its flying mode setting so that they got a much better view of the city. Now Harry and Aunty Dare could easily see all the sights of London. When they went inside the Houses of Parliament, Harry had so much fun running around all the corridors pulling faces at all the people who were just standing like statues. But eventually, it was time to go home, and they started to make their way back to Harry's home. It was at this point that Aunty Dare spotted something bad happening. There was a bank robbery taking place and the robbers were trying to steal the bank's money. When I say the bank's money, I mean the people's money really.

'What shall we do, Aunty, they can't get away with robbing the bank, it's other people's money like my daddy's,' said Harry.

'Quite right, Harry, well said,' replied Aunty Dare as she zoomed down to where the robbery was taking place and parked the scooter. 'Stay here, Harry, I won't be a moment,' she said.

Aunty Dare looked around the robbery scene and soon spotted the robbers' getaway car. She went up to it found the bonnet release catch, opened the bonnet then disconnected the battery. 'My, that will stop their little game,' she said to herself.

Then she tied the robbers' legs back to a guard rail which ran outside the bank. *That will trip you up, you naughty blighter,* she thought. With all that done, Aunty Dare then walked back to where Harry was standing.

'Can we call the police and let them know about this robbery?' asked Harry.

'Tip top idea, Harry, I'll send a message out using my Hypersonic Sentinel messaging mega drive app; it will be the very first thing that the police will hear when I reset the time,' said Aunty Dare.

Wow! Harry wasn't sure about how any of that would actually work, but he knew that Aunty Dare was the tops, so if she says it will happen, then it will just happen! Aunty Dare, she's so cool, thought Harry.

Chapter Three – Back Home

Eventually after all that excitement, Aunty Dare and Harry arrived back home. It had been an epic exciting day. Aunty Dare parked her scooter by the back door next to the kitchen where it was parked before they started their adventure.

'Right, Harry, I will need to reset time to bring everything back to normal. There's a timer here so I will set it to give ourselves 20 seconds to get into the house and into the front room. Then by the time we sit down on the armchairs, everything will be back to normal again. Remember, Harry, to sit on the right chair, it's important that you do that. Now, ready, steady, go, Harry, Harry, go!' And with that, Harry did as he was told. He ran straight through the back kitchen door; he saw that his mummy was standing like a statue in the kitchen and went straight into the front room and sat where his double was sitting on the armchair and waited for Aunty Dare. But where was she…

Harry needn't have worried, as a few seconds later Aunty Dare appeared; she sat down on the opposite armchair, raised her hand and said, 'And now, five, four, three, two, one,' and with a click of her fingers said, 'snap…'

'Oh, hello,' said Mrs Alliss popping her head around the front room door, 'I thought I heard you two chatting together. Now would you like that cup of tea I promised you, Aunty Dare?'

'Oh, yes, please,' said Aunty Dare, 'I'm rather parched, must be all that chatting with Harry. Well, I will have to leave you now, Harry, I mustn't get any of your germs, must I, you be good now.' And with that, she gave Harry that naughty wink of hers and followed Mrs Alliss into the kitchen.

'Bye, Aunty Dare, thank you for seeing me; it was great fun.'

Aunty Dare turned around and put her finger to her lips and quietly said, 'Shuuuuush.'

'Two sugars please, Nicola,' said Aunty Dare…

Harry and the Bad Neighbour

Chapter One – Harry Having a Think

Harry was in a thinking mood today. It was a Saturday morning and was a dull and rainy start to the day, so after Harry had some breakfast, he went back to his bedroom to have a little think. He sometimes liked to do that rather than watch TV with his brother, Hugo. He started by thinking about where he lived. Harry lived in what he thought was a very nice house, where he was very happy living with his mum and dad. The house was nice and warm, and it was a reasonable size to make it comfortable. Harry was sometimes quite surprised by some of his friends' homes. He naturally thought that they would be the same as his, but that wasn't always the case as some of them were, well, quite small really. That made him think that he was quite a lucky boy. Now the one thing that he really liked was that he had his own bedroom. His brother also had his own bedroom, and Harry was very happy with that because sometimes, like today, he wanted to be on his own to have a little think.

Harry knew that sharing a bedroom with his brother wasn't always the best thing. That's because his friend Billy had to share his bedroom with his younger brother Sammy, and that didn't always appear to work very well. His friend Billy was a tidy boy, but his brother Sammy wasn't! He would make a mess wherever he went. Billy would get quite cross at times because of it. Harry knew that when Billy came around to see him, he would have loved to have a bedroom like his.

Harry also had a nice garden where he could play football with his friends. It was nice and flat and was perfect for playing football. Harry was happy about that as one of his friends, Archie, had a garden that looked like a ski slope. It was hard playing football in that garden. If you kicked the ball too hard when you were at the top of the garden, it would go right to the bottom of the garden, and it was jolly hard work getting the ball back and running up the slope! Harry's daddy would say, 'Oh, yes, Harry, but look how strong your legs will be running up and down that garden.' But Harry wasn't so sure about that. His legs, he thought, were just fine as they were, whatever his daddy would say. Some of his friends would be so tired after running around in Archie's garden that they couldn't walk home. Harry liked his garden to be nice and flat!

Chapter Two – Neighbours

Harry had a nice neighbour on one side of the garden who was called Mr Kevin Keith. Harry would always call him Mr Keith and never Kevin. It's just as Mr Keith would like it. Mr Keith was a very nice man, and, he liked model boats. He had lots of them and would build his model boats in his garden shed. He would often let Harry and his friends play with some of these boats in the little lake in the local park. Harry liked the steam yacht that Mr Keith had built. It was quite a big model yacht, all made from wood. It was a bit tricky to get the steam engine to work as you had to light a little fire to make the steam. That always seemed a little bit dangerous to Harry, but Mr Keith didn't seem to have any problems lighting it. It would then puff smoke from its little chimney, and it had a whistle that made a "toot, toot" sound blowing little puffs of steam into the air. Everyone looked when that steam yacht cruised around the park lake; it was quite a sight.

That reminded Harry of an incident a little while back when Mr Keith and his daddy were both there. Another man came to the lake whom they had never seen before. He was carrying a model of a battleship that he had built. It was all in grey, and the man started to tell Mr Keith all about it. 'Yes, it's made of hi-tech materials, radio controlled of course, cost a fortune to make…' And on and on he went talking about his model boat.

Mr Keith just said, 'Well, be careful as my steam yacht only goes in one direction and I don't have any sort of control over it once it's in the water.'

'Well, if it hits my battleship, your little wooden tug will be just splinters on the water,' the man smugly said. Harry thought he was quite rude to Mr Keith. Well, it didn't all quite go to plan, Harry remembered. The man lost control of his battleship right in front of the stream yacht, which then hit it dead in the centre, or "amidship" as Mr Keith later explained. The battleship then flipped over, broke into two and sunk within less than a minute. Everyone looked in total surprise as it was expected that Mr Keith's wooden yacht would have sunk instead. Harry tried not to laugh as the man was such a big head, and now his model battleship was at the bottom of the lake sunk by a wooden tug as the man called it! Mr Keith just carried on as if nothing had happened.

But Harry liked the wind yacht best of all. It had a big sail, and when it was pushed into the water, it would catch the wind and make a long sweeping curve around the edge of the lake and end up where Harry had pushed it from. Harry thought that was very simple and very clever all at the same time. Mr Keith would buy Harry and his friends some ice cream from the little shop in the park and sit and smoke his pipe. Harry thought that Mr Keith looked like his model steam yacht with all the smoke coming out of his pipe!

On the other side of the garden was his other neighbour, Miss Ray. Now Harry didn't dislike Miss Ray, but Miss Ray didn't like Harry, well, she didn't like Hugo either or any of Harry's friends. One day, when they were all out playing football, she shouted out, 'YOU CHILDREN, STOP MAKING ALL THAT NOISE, WILL YOU!' It made them all jump and even Mr Keith was a bit surprised by all that shouting by Miss Ray. He even stopped smoking his pipe!

To try and be good neighbours and not have any bad feelings, Mrs Alliss spoke to Miss Ray about this saying they were only children playing in the garden. 'Well, if they want to play football, then they should go and use the park. Gardens are for contemplation,' said Miss Ray. She was quite a grumpy lady at times, and even Mrs Alliss thought she was being unreasonable.

Now Harry didn't understand what "contemplation" meant other than not being able to play football with his friends. So, Harry always had to wait until Miss Ray went out before he and Hugo and some of his friends could play football in the garden, without being shouted at that is!

The good news was that Miss Ray did go out a few times a week, and when she did, it was for a long time. Harry always knew when Miss Ray was going out as she would make a lot of noise driving her little car out of her driveway. She would always park it at the end of her driveway right up to her garage door, which sometimes she would bump into. Then when she wanted to go out, she had to drive the car all the way backwards down the driveway to get onto the main road. The engine would make a terrible noise as she would rev the engine very hard but at the same time go backwards ever so slowly.

'She'll burn the clutch out if she drives like that,' said Mr Alliss one day. Harry wasn't sure what "burn the clutch out" meant, but as he was a clever boy, he guessed that it meant that Miss Ray might break her car if she drives like that. Mr Keith would often say, 'If she drops the clutch, there's going to be one big accident if she drives like that!' Again, Harry didn't know what "drop the clutch" meant either, but he thought that Miss Ray might not be a very good driver. Harry wasn't sure what sort of car it was, but one of his friends said that he read a word on the car's rear boot lid. It said Nova.

'Do you think that Miss Ray's Nova is a strong car?' asked Hugo after Miss Ray had started another one of her little trips.

'Yes, I think it's a very, very strong car,' said Harry, 'because everyone thinks that it will breakdown one day, but it's still going!'

When Miss Ray went out, the boys would play football on the lawn. Mr Keith would often look over the fence and shout and cheer the boys on when they played. He loved watching football and his cheering made it all great fun. Mr Keith said he supported the Fleet. 'Well, someone has to,' he would say. Harry hadn't decided which team he was going to support, even though his daddy said he should support the Spurs. Harry wasn't sure, so he would have a little think about that too.

Chapter Three – The Accident

On this day, the boys were playing outside in the back garden when they heard Miss Ray return from one of her trips. 'Oh, no, Miss Ray is back,' said Hugo. 'She's back early,' said Harry, 'quick, let's hide behind the tree and see if she goes out again.'

They hid behind the large magnolia tree where they had a good view of Miss Ray's garage and back gate that Miss Ray would always walk through to get inside her house. Miss Ray never used the front door. Harry wondered why, but that's just the way it was. The back gate opened and Miss Ray walked towards her door carrying all her shopping in large bags, when suddenly she tripped. Down she went with a horrible crash of shopping spilling out and Miss Ray falling on the path. Then they heard Miss Ray give out a cry of pain and then nothing. Harry thought that he could hear Miss Ray moaning in pain so he turned around to his brother.

'Quick, Hugo, get Mummy, tell her that Miss Ray has had an accident,' said Harry.

'What are you going to do, Harry?' asked Hugo.

'I'm going to see if I can help her,' replied Harry.

'Be careful, Harry, she doesn't like us children,' said Hugo.

'Don't worry, if she gets angry, I can run faster than she can. Go, Hugo, be quick.' And with that, Hugo ran off to find their mummy, and Harry jumped over the garden fence and ran towards where Miss Ray was lying. When Harry arrived, he could see that Miss Ray was quietly moaning a little, but she wasn't moving. All the shopping had spilled out of the shopping bags and was lying on the ground. It was quite a mess.

'Are you all right, Miss Ray?' asked Harry. 'Can I do anything?' Miss Ray's head was lying on a box of eggs that had all broken, leaving her face full of eggy mess. It probably saved her head from being badly hurt, but it did look in a terrible state.

'Can you clean my face?' she said. 'The eggs are making my eyes sting.' Harry looked around him. The shopping was all over the path, but luckily, he spotted an unopened bottle of water. He thought that he would have to use all his strengthen to open the bottle as they were quite hard for children to open. Harry took a big breath and twisted the bottle cap…and hooray, it opened! Then looking around for some tissues, he saw some kitchen roll lying on the ground and tore a few sheets off.

Gently pouring the water over Miss Ray's face, he cleaned the egg mess from Miss Ray's eyes. It wasn't easy as there was a lot of eggy mess to clean off, but Miss Ray lay quite still which helped Harry to wash it all away. 'Thank you, child,' she said, 'that was very kind of you.'

'Can I do anything else?' asked Harry.

'Could you call an ambulance?' asked Miss Ray.

'I asked my brother Hugo to get our mummy; she should be here very soon,' he said.

'Thank you,' said Miss Ray. Harry held Miss Ray's hand. He had never seen a bad accident before so he didn't really know what to do, but he thought that holding her hand and just being there would be a comfort for her.

Chapter Four – The Ambulance Arrives

'Harry. Harry, where are you…' It was Mrs Alliss calling out.

'I'm here, Mummy, by Miss Ray's back door; come quick, Miss Ray needs an ambulance.'

Suddenly by the back gate, Mrs Alliss, Hugo and Mr Keith all appeared and took in the scene. There was Miss Ray lying on the ground face down. All her shopping was scattered everywhere and Harry was kneeling beside her trying to make her as comfortable as possible. Mr Keith came over and took one look at Miss Ray and said, 'Don't worry, Miss Ray, I'll call an ambulance.' And with that, he got out his mobile phone out and dialled 999.

'Hello…Yes…Ambulance please…yes, go to Number 8, Acacia Gardens, Brokenhamstead…Yes, no…Number 8…and please be quick, the lady has got concussion.' Mr Keith put his phone away. 'The ambulance is on its way,' he said then added, 'they didn't recognise the address at first, goodness me, what's the world coming to!'

Harry leaned over Miss Ray and said, 'It's all right, Miss Ray, the ambulance is coming now; it won't be long.'

'Thank you, child,' said Miss Ray with the remaining strength in her body. Harry could see that she was in a terrible state. They all then waited, listening for that distinctive sound of the ambulance siren. Fortunately, it wasn't that long before they heard the siren. As soon as Mr Keith heard it, he went out to the road to direct the ambulance to the accident.

'I'll be on the road to wave it down,' he said, 'we don't want to waste a minute.'

The ambulance arrived and parked outside Miss Ray's house. Harry could hear Mr Keith saying, 'This way, this way, she's over here.' The first paramedic came through the back gate and walked up to where Miss Ray was lying.

'What's this lady's name?' he asked.

'Miss Ray,' said Harry.

The paramedic knelt beside Miss Ray and said, 'Hello, darling, what's your first name?'

'Vanessa,' said Miss Ray.

'All right, Vanessa, don't worry, we'll soon have you all patched up.'

'Young man,' said Miss Ray, 'do we know each other?'

'No, darling,' said the paramedic with a wink.

'Well, kindly refer to me as Miss Ray from now on…thank you. Well, get on with it and get me to the hospital and be quick about it,' said Miss Ray.

That wasn't quite the response that anyone was expecting to hear from Miss Ray. Somewhat embarrassed, Mr Keith turned around to the paramedic and said, 'Sorry about that, she's in a bit of a state of shock; she doesn't mean anything by it.'

Well, Harry looked at the paramedic and the paramedic looked at Harry. They both had that knowing look, which meant that they knew exactly what Miss Ray meant! The paramedic was now joined by his partner and they gently moved Miss Ray onto a stretcher and started to make their way towards the ambulance when Miss Ray raised her arm and said, 'STOP.' Then pointing to Harry, she said, '…Come here, little boy.'

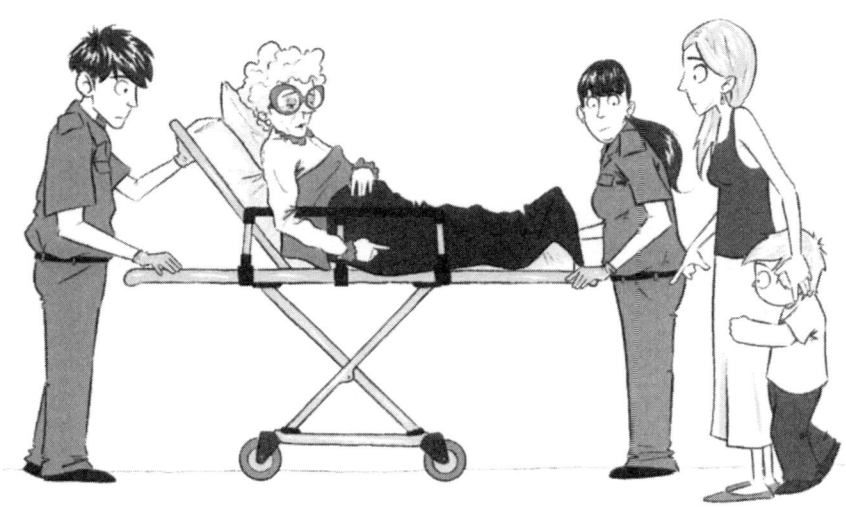

Harry looked at his mummy; he wasn't too sure what was going to happen next. But Mrs Alliss pushed him forward. Harry gingerly walked across to where Miss Ray was lying on the stretcher.

'What's your name, little boy?' asked Miss Ray.

'Harry, Miss,' he replied.

'Thank you, Harry, for helping me; I know a lot of people wouldn't have because I'm a grumpy old lady, but you did and I am very grateful to you. I would like to say sorry for how I have been to you, but I will try and make it up to you. Please play as much football as you like, it's only fair.'

Harry smiled; he felt relieved. 'That's all right, Miss Ray, I hope you feel better soon.' And with that, Miss Ray turned her head and pointed to the paramedic to move forward. The stretcher was slid into the back of the ambulance, and with its siren on, it made its way to the hospital.

'Well done, Harry,' said Mr Keith, 'that was a jolly brave thing for you to do. You kept her calm and that was a big help to the paramedics. That hopefully will be a very different Miss Ray when she comes back. She'll be all right; she's a lot tougher than she looks.'

'Yes, well done, Harry,' said Mrs Alliss, 'that was so brave of you; I'm so very proud of you.'

'Thank you,' said Harry beaming with pride.

Chapter Five – The Home Coming

It was three weeks to the day that Miss Ray came home from the hospital. Both Mr and Mrs Alliss and Mr Keith had regularly visited Miss Ray over that time. She was quite overcome by how people seemed to care about her.

'You silly moo,' Mr Keith said in his jovial way on one of the visits, 'of course we all care.'

Harry was a bit surprised when he heard that, but Mrs Alliss said that Miss Ray took it all in good humour. *Not something I would have done*, thought Harry to himself.

It was around eleven o'clock in the morning that Mr Keith arrived with Miss Ray. He had picked her up in his car from the hospital and took her home. When she got out of the car, she was a little bit unsteady on her legs so Mr Keith gave her his arm to steady herself, and then they both slowly walked towards Harry's house. On ringing the doorbell, Mrs Alliss opened the door and greeted Miss Ray.

'Hello, Vanessa, so glad you've come home at last, come in and I'll make a nice pot of tea for as all,' she said.

'Is Harry in?' enquired Miss Ray.

'Yes, he is.' And Mrs Alliss called out to Harry expecting him to be upstairs in his bedroom, but Harry popped his head out of the front room with a cheeky impish smile on his face. He's caught his mummy out he thought to himself.

'Hmmm,' said Mrs Alliss, 'I thought you were upstairs, Harry, still never mind please take Miss Ray into the front room and we'll all have some tea and cake.'

'Oh, can we have some chocolate brownies?' asked Harry.

'That would be nice; they are my favourites as well,' said Miss Ray. Luckily, Mrs Alliss had baked a fresh lot of brownies for Harry the day before, so chocolate brownies it was. Once the tea had been made and they were all seated, Miss Ray turned to Harry and took out a parcel wrapped up in tissue paper and gave it to him. 'There you are, Harry, that's for you for helping and saving me. Go on, please open it,' she said.

Harry unwrapped the parcel to find a football shirt with a Number 10 on it with his name on the back. Funnily enough, it was a Spurs shirt! 'Thank you, Miss Ray, did Daddy help you with getting this shirt for me?' asked Harry.

'Yes, he did, when he popped in to visit me at hospital, he said it was your favourite team, is that right, Harry?'

Harry smiled. 'Oh, yes, thank you, Miss Ray.' He knew that it was his daddy's way of being a little bit cheeky, because it was his favourite football team, but it didn't matter.

'Oh, and this as well,' continued Miss Ray, 'I heard that you liked magic, Harry, so I got you a Rubik's cube.' Now in case that you don't know a Rubik's cube is a cube that is made up of many separate-coloured cubes and the trick is to get all the same colours on each face of the big cube. It's quite tricky to do and can take some people hours and hours to do. Some people can't do it at all!

'Let me show you how to do it,' said Miss Ray, and she took the cube, and in a few short moments, she had all the same colours on all the sides of the cube. Everyone was totally amazed how quickly Miss Ray did it. 'There, that's good magic,' said Miss Ray. 'You try, Harry.'

'Can I wait till Aunty Dare comes to see me this afternoon and I'll do it with her; it will be fun doing it with her,' said Harry.

'Yes, that will be fun,' said Miss Ray, 'but let me know if you need any help.'

'Oh, I will, Miss Ray, don't worry, I will.' *But I don't think so*, thought Harry to himself…

Harry and the Train Ride

Chapter One – Catching the Train

Why is it that parents make you go to sleep when you are not tired and then wake you up when you are still asleep and then say things like, "Lovely morning, Harry"? *How do I know what sort of morning it is; I haven't got out of bed yet!* mused Harry.

It was Saturday morning and Mr Alliss was super excited. He was going to take Harry and Hugo for a train ride. Harry wasn't that keen himself as the trains he went on with his mummy were normally very busy with lots of people standing up and sometimes even pushing you. It was all right for them, but when you're small, it's not so much fun living with giants, thought Harry.

'Looking forward to today, Harry?' quizzed Mr Alliss.

'So, so,' replied Harry not sounding too enthusiastic. 'What's for breakfast, Daddy?'

'Oh, don't worry about breakfast, we'll have a little bit of cereal and then we'll go. We can get a proper breakfast on the train,' said Mr Alliss excitedly. After the boys had finished their cereal, they had to quickly put their coats on and walk briskly to the station.

'Is this where we are going on the train, Daddy?' asked Harry.

'Oh, no, we have to go to the main line station for that train, this is just the loop line to where we need to get to,' replied Mr Alliss.

'Why…why can't the train be at our station?' exclaimed Harry; after all, it made a lot more sense to him. Hugo nodded, he thought so as well. Both boys weren't quite as enthusiastic as their daddy, that's for sure!

'Well, it's just the way it is, Harry, chip, chip, we best get a jiggle on otherwise we might miss our connection,' said Mr Alliss. They all had to walk a little bit faster than normal to catch the train which would take them to the main line station, and that was quite tiring first thing in the morning especially after breakfast! The loop line train arrived on time and the three of them got on. *Hooray*, thought Harry, *at least we have an empty train and there are seats we can all sit together on.* That cheered Harry up, and the train wasn't too smelly either and that made a nice change. It took a long while to get to the other station, or so it seemed to Harry. There wasn't much to see out of the windows and his daddy was too busy reading his train book to talk.

'What's your book about, Daddy, is it about the train we are going to see?' asked Harry.

'Yes,' replied Mr Alliss and he kept on reading his book. He really didn't want to be disturbed.

Oh, how boring thought Harry, and he put his head in his hands and thought how he could have played with his Scalextric set or rode his bike in the garden or played football with his friends. It all seemed more fun than going to see a train! Eventually, they arrived at the Main Station. Harry thought that they must have walked for miles and miles through the long winding corridors just to get to the platform.

'Here you are, Harry, this is your ticket, and here you are, Hugo, this is your ticket. We must put it through that ticket machine to let us through the barrier,' said Mr Alliss. They all put their tickets through the ticket machine, Hugo first then Harry and then Mr Alliss. 'Okay, follow me,' said Mr Alliss and led the group towards the train which was standing at the platform.

'Aren't we getting into the carriage?' asked Harry.

'No, not yet,' said Mr Alliss, 'we'll look at the locomotive first.' Well, they finally arrived by the locomotive. There were lots of other Mr Allisses looking at the locomotive as well. Then Harry saw a nameplate on the side of the engine.

'Mallard, is that the name of this train?' asked Harry.

'Yes,' said Mr Alliss, 'isn't she beautiful?'

'What's a Mallard?' asked Harry.

'Well, actually, it's a duck,' said Mr Alliss.

'But it's a train,' said Harry looking a bit confused.

'Well, it's a locomotive actually, and I know it does sound a little bit strange to call it after a duck, but everything has to have a name and this train's name is Mallard just like your name is Harry,' explained Mr Alliss. Both boys looked at their daddy and then at each other. It didn't really make a lot of sense to them, but they hoped that breakfast would come soon; they were so hungry!

'Come on, we can't stand here much longer as the train is going to go in a few minutes, let's find our seats.' And with that, they got into the first carriage just behind the engine. It wasn't the same sort of carriage that they had on the loop line train. The seats were very big and comfortable, a bit like armchairs in their home. They all sat together and had a big table in front of them as well as little lights that they could turn on if they wanted to.

A man came up to where they were seated and asked, 'Are you ready to order breakfast, sir?'

'Yes, please, may I have three full English breakfasts with baked beans and sausages and tomatoes. Oh, and a pot of tea for three as well. Is that all right, boys?' said Mr Alliss.

'Yes, please,' they both replied. Harry's tummy started to rumble thinking of all that lovely food.

'Very well, sir, won't be long, just as soon as the train gets going. I'll bring the tea…milk and sugar, everyone?' The train pulled away from the station with clouds of steam and smoke going past the windows. Everyone in their carriage was so excited when they started moving, they were all saying Mallard this and Mallard that and looking at various books and exchanging pictures of trains. They all seemed very excited by it all.

Harry and Hugo just waited for their breakfasts!

The waiter eventually came with a tray full of food. 'There you are, gents, be careful the plates are very hot. Enjoy,' said the waiter. He seemed to be the only grown up on the train who didn't appear to be very excited about being on this train, thought Harry! After breakfast, which was delicious, the plates were cleared away, and Harry asked where the toilet was.

'Waiter, where are the toilets, please?' asked Mr Alliss.

'At the end of the carriage on the left, just push the door in. It's vacant now if you need to use it,' said the waiter helpfully. Harry made his way to the end of the carriage. Everyone around him were chatting way about trains this and signals that and rails this and rails that. *I don't get that excited when I play with my train set*, Harry thought to himself. Harry was then just about to open the door to the toilet when suddenly the train went through a tunnel and it all got very dark. He stood still and waited till the lights went back on or the train reached the end of the tunnel.

Chapter Two – The Wizard

In a few moments, it was light again; the train was travelling quite fast now going clickety clack, clickety clack; it was making quite a noise. But then Harry noticed that everyone in the carriage had suddenly disappeared, where had they gone? Harry ran back to where his daddy and Hugo sat, and they were gone too! Where could they be, where was everyone?

Now Harry was a brave boy so he kept calm and thought that there must be a good reason for this. I mean nobody just disappears into thin air do they! He would have called his mummy, but only his daddy had a phone and he was no longer there. So, Harry made his way to the next carriage along. He opened the connecting doors between the carriages and went in…nothing, it was empty as well.

He ran down the carriage corridor to the next carriage, opened the connecting doors and went inside the third carriage. Nothing…nobody was here either! Yet all these carriages were full of people before. Harry went into the last carriage on the train and again the same thing; it was empty too, but the train was going faster and faster and the clickety clack noise was getting louder and louder. Harry ran back to the first carriage, opened the carriage door and then stopped in his tracks. There at the front of the carriage was standing what he could only describe as a small wizard-looking person. He was very stooped, wore a cape over his shoulders, his face had a very scraggy beard; he had big scary eyes and didn't appear to have all his teeth; he also wore a very funny pointy hat, and probably most importantly of all, he didn't look very friendly at all!

'Hello, Harry, I've been waiting for you, where have you been?' asked the wizard in a very menacing way.

'I've been looking for my daddy and brother and the other people on the train,' said Harry. 'Did you make them disappear; what have you done with them?'

'Nothing,' said the wizard, 'or at least nothing for you to worry about for the moment that is, unless of course you don't tell me where the secret of the Efil is.'

'The secret of Efil? I don't know anything about any such secret,' said Harry with a horrible feeling of despair. He was starting to get very worried as he really didn't understand what was going on.

'Come, come, Harry, you are like me, you are a sorcerer and I want your magical powers and then I will be like you if I get the secret of Efil,' said the wizard. Harry was perplexed, why did the wizard think he was a sorcerer and why did he want to be like him he thought to himself, but he knew he had to do something and quickly as this wizard didn't look friendly and he had to save his daddy and brother and the other people on the train.

'Psst, psst,' said a little voice behind Harry. He looked around and saw a little girl who looked a little bit like the fairy that is put on top of their family Christmas tree. 'Oh, she won't save you, Harry; she's lost all her powers; only I can save you, Harry, if you give me the secret of Efil,' said the wizard.

Harry walked towards the wizard and stopped by where Hugo and his daddy once sat. The seats were empty, but on one of the seats he saw his daddy's train notebook. The wizard hadn't noticed this book so Harry made to sit down on the book and then carefully put it inside his pocket.

'If I give you the secret of the Efil, will you promise to bring back my daddy and my brother?' asked Harry.

'Yes, of course,' said the wizard, but Harry still felt very unsure; he didn't trust him. Harry now had a plan, so he took the book out of his pocket and placed it on the table.

'Here it is,' said Harry, 'this is the book with the secret of Efil.'

The fairy was now standing behind Harry and whispered, 'Get the black ring from his finger, he needs that ring. Without the ring, the spell will go and all the people will come back, be very careful.'

'Very well, Wizard, I will give you the book if you return my daddy and my brother and bring all the people back,' said Harry.

'Don't trust him,' whispered the fairy.

'But,' Harry continued, 'if I give you the book, let me have a look at that ring you are wearing.'

'Why? Why do you want to see my ring, little boy?' asked the wizard suspiciously.

'Because it's so shiny and the black colour is so deep; I've never seen such a ring,' said Harry innocently.

'Give me the book first,' said the wizard thinking that at last the secret of the Efil was now within his grasp.

'No, we give the book and the ring together,' said Harry, hoping that his plan would work.

Harry held out the book, but the wizard snatched it from his grasp, but luckily, the fairy distracted the wizard for a moment and Harry grabbed his hand and pulled the ring off his finger.

'Ouch,' said the wizard, rubbing his ring finger. Harry had to use all his strength to pull it off, but he now had it in his hand. 'Very well, little boy, look at my ring, but it is of no use to you, now where is the secret of Efil?'

'Turn to the page marked Mallard,' said Harry.

The wizard pored over the pages until he found Mallard, which was marked with a yellow post it notes that Mr Alliss had marked the page with.

'Ah ha,' he proclaimed triumphantly, 'but what does Loco 4-6-2 mean, what is that code for; don't trifle with me, little boy; I think you are trying to cheat me,' he said angrily.

'It's Mallard's train number,' shouted Harry, and with that, he opened the train's top window and thew the ring out.

'Noooo!' screamed the wizard. 'My ring, my ring…I need my ring.' But now, the wizard suddenly started to shake and at the same time started to shrink, becoming smaller and smaller and smaller right in front of Harry. 'I'll get you for this,' he squeaked as he was losing his voice as well, but Harry didn't care as the wizard was losing his power just as the fairy had said he would. Soon the wizard had become a small fly and flew out of the train's window.

It will be all right now,' said the fairy, 'everything will return to normal very soon; your daddy and brother will reappear, I promise.'

'But what about you?' asked Harry.

'Oh, don't worry, I must return, I must save other people from the evil wizard. It's what I have been chosen to do, but don't forget me, Harry.'

'I'll never do that…what's your name…?' Harry asked, but it was too late the fairy had disappeared just as quietly as she first appeared. The train started to shake violently; everything was crashing around Harry; he felt the train slowing down, and then suddenly, all the lights went out. It became very dark. Harry held onto the table and just closed his eyes. He wished that everything would go back to as it was with his daddy and Hugo safely back…

'There you are, Harry,' said Mr Alliss, 'I wondered where you had got to. Okay, it's my turn to use the toilet now, is it all right to use it?' Harry got out of his seat and went over and gave his daddy a big hug, a super squeeze, in fact.

'Yes, Daddy, it's fine,' said Harry so relieved that everything was back to normal.

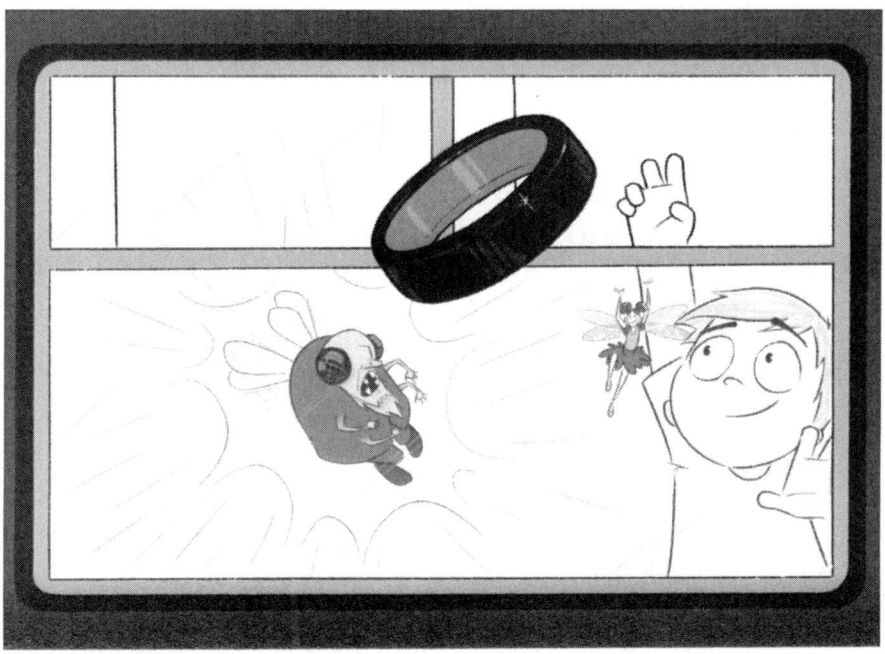

Mr Alliss wasn't expecting quite such a reaction from Harry and was taken a bit aback, but he gave his son the same hug back. Harry was always full of surprises thought Mr Alliss but that's one of the many reasons that we all love him so much.

'Are you okay, Harry?' asked Hugo. 'Did something happen back there?'

'Yes and yes,' answered Harry. Hugo knew that something had happened, but he was sure that Harry would tell him later.

'I am so glad you got us all back, Harry,' said Hugo.

Harry and the Lightning Pilot

Chapter One – The Robbery

It was a nice sunny morning when Harry woke up. It was Tuesday so Harry got dressed in his school uniform ready for another day. Harry loved going to school and he really liked his teacher Mrs Alex. He would always walk to school with his brother Hugo and his friends Isla and Cameron. They would laugh and chat about what they did at school and the school work they must do. On this morning, Harry decided to leave a little bit earlier than usual after he had his breakfast. He said his goodbyes to his mummy who gave him a kiss, but before he started to walk to school, Mrs Alliss said, 'Hugo isn't quite ready yet, Harry, will you wait for him with your friends by the post box and I'll bring him to you.'

'Yes, Mummy, I will,' said Harry. Harry did a last-minute check that he had everything in his satchel, especially his lunch. He loved his mummy's packed lunches, as did all his friends. He was always sharing his lunchbox with them. Harry was a bit of a feeder. When he got to the post box where he was going to wait for his brother, he suddenly heard someone shouting.

'Get off me, get off,' shouted the old man, 'leave me alone, HELP ME someone, HELP ME…'

Harry looked and saw three older boys trying to rob an old gentleman on the street. Harry didn't hesitate; he knew that he had to help the old man. He looked around him and saw some of his friends making their way to school. He shouted at the top of his voice 'Cameron, Isla, Freddie, Jamie, Bertie, help me…' Then without waiting, he charged at the boys who were trying to rob the old man. 'GET AWAY!' he shouted at the top of his voice. 'GET AWAY!'

His friends saw what Harry was doing so they knew they had to help immediately. They charged down the road shouting at the top of their voices. 'GET AWAY, GET AWAY…' They all made a lot of noise, and I mean a lot! The robbers looked at all the children running towards them and decided it was time to leave. It may also have been because a police car came around the corner just at that very moment as well that may have scared them off. Harry arrived by the poor old man who was lying on the road. There was a bit of blood coming from his face. His nose was bleeding.

'Are you all right, sir?' said Harry.

'Yes, thank you, young man, thank you for shouting at those awful boys; you must have frightened them off.'

WPC Hillary Evans Number 111 got out of her patrol car and came up to where Harry and the old gentleman were. 'Are you all right, sir?' she asked. 'I will call you an ambulance, I think you may need some first aid.' Then turning to Harry, WPC Evans continued. 'That was a very brave thing to do, but you really should have called the police first and not tried to help. In this case, you did very well. Your friends helped as well. That was very brave of you all,' she said looking at all the children who by now were all standing by the unfortunate old gentleman.

In a few moments' time, the ambulance arrived and the old gentleman was taken away. He wasn't too badly hurt and Harry was glad about that. WPC Evans asked Harry for his address in case she needed to contact his mummy about what had just happened. She thanked all the children and asked them to go to school now.

'Have a good day, children,' she said. '…Well done and stay safe.'

Just before WPC Evans was about to leave, Mrs Alliss arrived with Hugo. She asked what had happened and all the children started to speak at once telling what had happened. All that Mrs Alliss could hear was "Harry this" and "Harry that" and she couldn't make head nor tail of it at all.

'STOP, children, STOP!' called out WPC Evans. 'Let me explain.' And she calmly retold what had happened after she realised that she was talking to Harry's mummy. Mrs Alliss was a bit overwhelmed and gave Harry a big hug and thanked all the children for helping. She also thought all the children were very brave, very brave indeed!

Chapter Two – Meeting Roy

Harry had a good day at school and told his teacher Mrs Alex all about what had happened. All the children in the class thought that Harry was a hero. Harry was very proud that he did the right thing. When he went home, he spoke to his mummy about what had happened today.

'I know, Harry, WPC Evans came around to see me and she told me everything. That was very brave of you and your friends, but you must call the police next time,' said Mrs Alliss. Harry wondered how he could do that as he didn't have a phone nor did any of his friends. But he was sure that his mummy was right.

'Now go and do your school work, Harry, and I'll call you when your tea is ready,' said Mrs Alliss. She really was just so happy that Harry was safe and sound and not hurt in the incident. Harry went to his bedroom and started working on his project that his teacher had given to all the children. It was about flying and airplanes, which is a subject he loved. It was at this time that he heard the front door knocker sound and someone talking. Then his mummy shouted out, 'Harry, come downstairs please.'

Harry didn't know what this was all about, so he put his pencil and crayons down and went downstairs. Imagine his surprise when he walked into the front room to see the old gentleman he helped this very morning. The old gentleman stood up very straight and saluted Harry. He was a very distinguished looking gentleman. 'Hello, Harry, my name is Roy. I've come to say thank you, young sir, for helping me this morning. It could have turned out nasty if you and your friends hadn't helped me, no matter what that police lady might have said,' said Roy.

Harry could see that Roy was all right, but he had a bruise on his face. 'Sit down please,' said Harry, 'are you all right now?'

'Yes, thank you, a little bit bruised and my pride dented but nothing broken,' said Roy. 'I don't want to interrupt you, Harry; I know that you have some school work to do; I just wanted to say thank you for what you did today.'

'That's all right, I don't mind; I was running out of ideas in any case,' said Harry. 'I have to do a school project about flying and old airplanes; it's very interesting really, but I need more airplane stuff.'

'I was a pilot once,' said Roy.

'Wow,' said Harry, 'I've never met a pilot before, what did you fly?'

'An English Electric Lightning,' said Roy.

Well, Harry had never heard of an English Electric Lightning, but it sounded fantastic.

'What was that?' asked Harry.

'It was the fastest jet that we in the Air Force ever flew,' said Roy wistfully. 'It was all in silver and it looked like a rocket with wings.' Roy had a glint in his eyes recalling his memories.

'Gosh,' said Harry, 'do you have a picture of it?'

'Actually, yes, I have.' And Roy took out an old photo that was rather tatty and a bit dog eared, but it showed this amazing looking airplane. It was all in silver and really did look like a rocket with wings. Even though it was a very old photograph, the aircraft looked like it was very modern.

'Did you fly that? How fast did it go?' asked Harry; he was totally taken aback by what he was looking at.

'Yes, it was ever so fast. It was all very, very exciting, but I was a young man then and it was a great time to be young. Can you believe that that jet was able to fly at over a thousand miles per hour!' said Roy.

Now Harry couldn't imagine how fast a thousand miles per hour was, but it sounded fantastical! He kept looking at the photograph and could also see a car parked close by to where the Lightning was standing.

'What's that car?' asked Harry.

'That's my old Jensen Interceptor,' said Roy.

An English Electric Lightning and a Jensen Interceptor. Wow, what fantastic names thought Harry, this was just too amazing to take in. Harry never knew that these things ever existed and here was an old gentleman who flew this jet and drove this car and was telling him the story about them!

'I won't keep you now, Harry, I better go,' said Roy. The old gentleman went to leave and then he turned around and said to Harry, 'I've still got my old Jensen, if your mum and dad agree, I'll come around and show it to you.'

'Oh, yes, please,' said Harry; that was the best thing he had heard all day, even though he really liked being at school!

'Mummy, please will that be all right?' asked Harry. Mrs Alliss just nodded her head; she thought Roy was sweet and she could see just how excited Harry was by the prospect of going in the Jensen.

Chapter Three – The Test Drive

Well in a few days' time and with permission from Harry's parents, Roy arrived with his Jensen Interceptor. When Harry saw it, he was totally bowled over. 'Gosh,' said Harry, 'it's a fantastic car; it looks so fast!' Harry was amazed how it looked with its long bonnet and huge curved back window. It was low and sleek and looked like nothing that Harry had ever seen before. Its engine made a deep rumbling sound, making it sound powerful, and Harry could feel the heat coming from under the bonnet where the engine was. It was all a little bit too much to take in at once.

'If it's all right, ma'am,' said Roy to Mrs Alliss, 'I'll take Harry for a quick drive around the block. We won't go far.' Harry got into the Jenson sitting in the back seat and Roy started to move off. The car made a woofing noise from its powerful engine. 'Don't worry, Harry,' said Roy, 'this traffic is a bit heavy, but I'll turn off here and it will be a lot better.' They turned into a little road with a white gate that went across it; as the car approached it, it automatically opened and they drove straight on…

Suddenly, there were no cars anywhere, all the houses and pavements had all disappeared; there was only the countryside and a long straight road ahead of them. Harry wasn't sitting in the back of the car anymore but in the front passenger seat, but how did that happen!

"Whoosh…" and the car leapt forward; it went so fantastically fast, and then suddenly everything changed again, they were flying! The Jensen was no longer a car but a jet fighter and Roy was dressed in a pilot's suit with a helmet on as was Harry. They were flying in the Lightning!

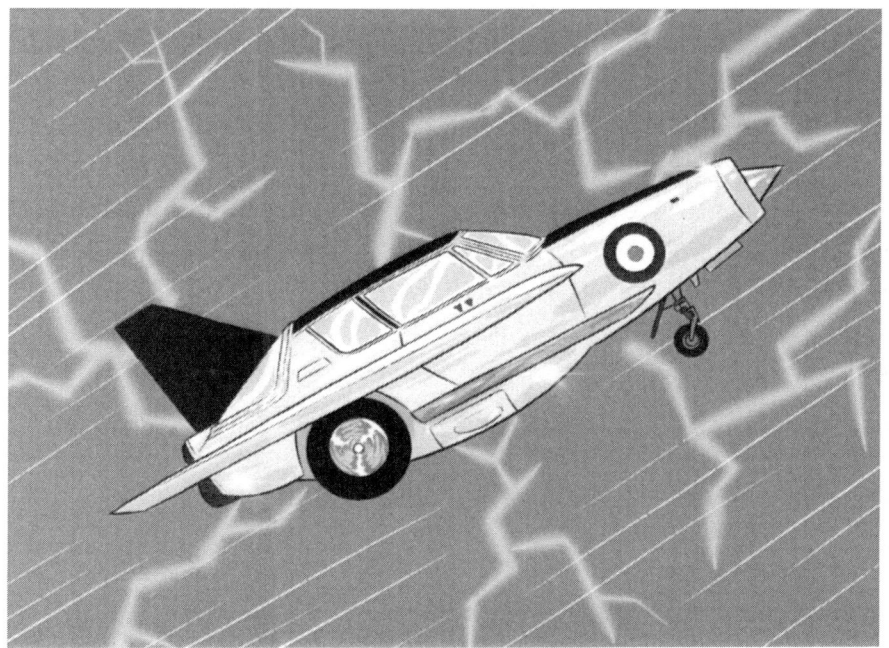

'What do you think of her?' asked Roy. 'She looks good, doesn't she?' But Harry just couldn't speak.

'…Roger Hotel, Alfa, Romeo, Romeo, Yankee, you are cleared for flight sequence 005, Angels 1, 7, 5, zero, zero, zero. Good luck,' said the voice in Harry's helmet.

'Okay, we are cleared to go, and we're off,' said Roy cheerfully.

'…Look out for Echo, Tango, Yankee, Papa, Echo, on your Port beam…call sign JAG,' said the voice again. 'Roger that Control,' said Roy in a calm and measured voice.

'That means we have another jet somewhere to our left, Harry,' explained Roy. Harry turned around and saw that Roy was no longer the old gentleman he knew but looked like a much, much younger man. A young Roy! Roy gave Harry a big thumbs up and Harry did the same. They were flying towards space and they could see the Earth starting to fall below them.

'It looks pretty up here,' said Roy, but Harry was still unable to speak until he eventually asked.

'What is that stick you are holding, where's the steering wheel gone?'

'That's the control stick, Harry; it's called a joystick and it controls the plane. Look, you take control now, gently does it,' said Roy.

Harry gently took hold of the joystick that was in front of him. 'You are a natural, Harry, just a light touch, that will do it. Now move the stick to the right, gently does it,' said Roy. Harry moved the stick gently to the right and the big jet turned to the right. It was so easy and the Lightning just responded to Harry's every control.

'Good, you're flying it now, Harry, you'll make a great pilot; now move the stick to the left.' Harry moved the joystick to the left and the jet again responded and turned to the left. 'Great stuff, that's what we call banking, Harry, when you move to the right or to the left. You've got control, move the throttle levers and we'll see just how fast she really goes. It's the big black lever on your left, just push it forward as far as it will go,' said Roy. Harry did as he was told and the Lightning leapt forward; it was so fast that Harry felt himself being pushed into his seat. Could this be really happening though, Harry, could it, could it?

'Over there, Harry, look the International Space Station,' said Roy. Harry quickly looked around, but he missed it. 'Oh, can we go around again? I didn't really get a proper look,' asked Harry.

'No problem Harry, we'll whizz around again and take another look; it won't take long,' said Roy; he was really enjoying himself as well. They flew around the Earth looking at the different colours and continents that made up the blue planet. It was just amazing to see it all. Before very long, Roy said, 'Okay, Harry, we'll have to slow down now or we'll miss the space station, pull the throttle right back, Harry…no, a bit more…that's it, right back till it clicks shut.'

Harry did as he was told and felt the lever go "Click" as the Lightning slowed down till they were flying side by side with the space station. Harry waved to the crew in the space station; they waved back, but they were all a bit surprised by what they saw. How many times does a spaceman or woman see an English Electric Lightning flying alongside the space station, I ask you!

Hello, Hotel, Alfa, Romeo, Romeo, Yankee, time to come back to base,' the voice in their helmets told them.

'Roger Control, Willco,' said Roy.

'Okay, that means we must go home, Harry, have you enjoyed yourself; do you like flying the Lightning?' Harry was a bit lost for words; after all, it was so much to take in; all he could only say was one word…

'A…MA…ZING.'

The Lightning headed back towards Earth, and soon, they were getting ready to land on the same road that Harry recognised from which they had taken off from. 'We're here, Harry, get ready for touch down, pull the red lever down to lower the wheels,' said Roy. The wheels went down with a heavy "K…LUNK" sound. They were down and locked in position.

The Lightning landed with a big BANG as all its wheels touched the ground; it then slowed down incredibility quickly. It made Harry close his eyes for a few seconds, but when he opened them, he was no longer in the Lightning jet but back in the Jensen Interceptor. How did that happen! They came up to the same white gate that they drove through before, but this time, it didn't open automatically. Roy had to brake hard to avoid crashing into the gate. 'Oh dear, it gets stuck sometimes, Harry. I think next time I'll have to oil the hinges,' said Roy.

Slowly, the gates opened, and then, they were back on the same busy road that they had been driving on when they had left Harry's home. Roy just turned the corner and there was Harry's house. 'I'll wait for you to get inside, Harry, but we must do this again,' said Roy. 'Oh, yes, please. Bye, Roy, and thank you so much,' said Harry.

'No problem, young man, I'm glad it was such fun; you're a pilot now, Harry, you have got your wings,' said Roy. Just before Harry got out of the Jensen, he noticed that Roy was now looking like the old gentleman that he knew before. Where did the young Roy go…still no matter?

'Bye,' said Harry as he shut the car door behind him. He ran up to the front door and pressed the doorbell. Mrs Alliss came and opened the door. Waving goodbye to Roy as he drove off in his Jensen, Mrs Alliss said, 'My that was quick, Harry, did you enjoy the drive?'

'Oh, yes, Mummy,' said Harry, 'it was super, fantastic, awesome, amazing.'

'Well, you sound like you certainly enjoyed that, Harry, but next time invite Roy back into the house for a cup of tea,' said Mrs Alliss, 'and cake as well.'

'I will, Mummy, but have you heard of the International Space Station?' asked Harry.

Mrs Alliss thought for a short while, looked at Harry as mummies often do at their sons and then said, 'Yes, I think so, Harry, but why do you ask?'

'Oh, no reason, Mummy, what's for tea? I'm so hungry…

Harry and the Boy in the Tree

Chapter One – Difficult Times

Harry woke up as normal and got himself dressed. His brother Hugo was still asleep so he was quiet as not to wake him. Harry then went to the bathroom and brushed his teeth and washed his face. Standing at the top of the stairs, he heard his mummy and daddy talking. He wasn't sure, but it seemed that his mummy was crying. Then suddenly, his daddy appeared at the bottom of the stairs. 'Good morning, Harry,' said Mr Alliss.

'Hello, Daddy, are you going to work?' asked Harry.

'Yes, take care of your mummy and be a good boy, Harry,' said Mr Alliss.

'I will, Daddy, love you,' said Harry.

'Love you too, Harry.' And with that, Mr Alliss opened the front door to leave and closed it behind him.

Harry walked down the stairs and into the kitchen and saw his mummy; she looked very upset. He went up to her and gave her a cuddle. 'Are you all right, Mummy?' asked Harry.

'Yes. I'm fine,' said his mummy. Now Harry knew that if his mummy was crying and said that she's fine, then there must be something wrong. His best friend Isla told him that mummies don't cry for no reason. 'Can I do anything, Mummy?' he said.

'Harry, I need to tell you something,' said Mrs Alliss. Harry now felt a little bit worried, it's not normal for his mummy to speak to him like this.

'Is it bad?' he asked.

'Sadly, it's not good, we may have to move as your daddy is having some problems with work and we can't pay the mortgage,' said Mrs Alliss. Now Harry didn't understand what that really meant, what's a mortgage he thought, but he understood that they may have to move. That upset Harry, he loved his house and his garden and where he lived and the school he went to. Everything that Harry knew he really loved.

'Can I help?' said Harry.

'No, darling,' said Mrs Alliss, 'but we may have to put a "For Sale" sign on this house, that's why I needed to tell you so that it wouldn't come as a surprise to you. You're a big boy now, Harry, and these things happen, but we will cope. Don't worry, Harry, we have each other and that's all that matters. I'll make you some breakfast, what would you like…?'

Chapter Two – The Boy in the Tree

After breakfast, Mrs Alliss said that whilst she got herself and Hugo ready and dressed for Harry to go into the garden and play. Harry had a favourite spot in the garden. It was where a big tree grew and he would sit on a bench by the tree and chat to the tree sometimes. It made him happy as the tree was a friendly tree in Harry's world. He sat on the bench and told the tree what his mummy had said to him, when suddenly out of nowhere a boy appeared in front of him. He wasn't a boy that he recognised and his clothes were not the same as Harry normally wore.

'Hello, Harry,' said the boy. 'I'm the boy who lives in this tree.'

'I've never seen you before,' said Harry.

'No,' said the boy, 'that's because I'm the ghost in the tree.'

Now Harry wasn't sure what a ghost was, but for some reason, he wasn't scared. The boy looked friendly and Harry was sure he was a good ghost. 'Look, try and shake my hand,' said the boy as he reached this hand out to shake hands with Harry.

Harry took the boy's hand, but his hand just couldn't hold on to it! The boy laughed. 'See, you can't hold onto me as I'm a ghost.' Harry laughed as well. They were becoming friends as they spoke; it was as if Harry always knew the boy and the boy always knew Harry.

'My name is Harry.'

'I know,' said the boy. 'My name is Ethelred. I've heard you talking to the tree, Harry, that's why I know you. I wish I could play with you and your friends, but I'm a ghost so I can't. I didn't want to frighten you so I didn't appear until now. I feel that now is the right time.'

Now Harry knew that being a ghost meant that you must have had been a proper boy sometime, so he asked Ethelred what happened to him. 'My name is Ethelred, and my parents were forced out of our home by these knights a long, long time ago. We lived in a nice manor house, but the King of England didn't like my father, as he disagreed with what the king was doing to the people of England. My father was a good man, and he would look after the people who worked for him, but the king thought that he was giving too many freedoms to the people so he had him arrested and thrown out of our home. We lost everything; it was very difficult for us, as nobody would help us in case the king would punish them as well. So, we built a treehouse and had to live in it. It was a difficult time and life was very hard. One day, my parents had to go and find some food, but they never came back. I was left on my own. I waited and waited and prayed and prayed for their safe return, but they never came back. I tried looking for them, but I never found out what happened to them. Nobody would help me so I had to steal food to survive. It was a very bad time, Harry. I became weak and ill and died as there was nobody to look after me. I was buried here, but I was never given a proper burial so my spirit was never laid to rest. The tree we lived in was cut down, but this tree, your tree, Harry, was planted in more or less the same spot as our old treehouse, so I adopted it and that's why I'm this tree's ghost.' Harry thought that was a very, very sad story. He looked at Ethelred and saw that he had tears in his eyes.

'Don't worry, Harry, nobody can hurt me now,' said Ethelred. 'But before I can go to see my mother and father again, I have been told that I must do a really good deed, then my spirit will be released and I will be set free to meet them again. I heard you talk about your mummy crying, Harry, I think I can help you and your parents.'

'How?' asked Harry.

'You have to find the jewels that my father hid from the king,' said Ethelred.

'But why didn't you use the jewels to buy another house and food?' asked Harry.

'Because we were in hiding, Harry, if the jewels were found, we would be found as well and the king would show us no mercy,' said Ethelred.

'That's so sad, Ethelred; it's not fair,' Harry said in almost a whisper.

'Life isn't always fair, Harry, you have to learn that, but the jewels will help your family so much, and I want to give them to you, Harry,' said Ethelred.

'How can I find them?' asked Harry.

'They are buried in this garden somewhere; all I know is that you need to walk 20 paces or so from where our old tree house was and then dig in the centre of the garden,' said Ethelred.

Now Harry thought that this could be somewhere in the middle of the lawn and that might upset his daddy. Ethelred saw that Harry was troubled. 'Don't worry, Harry, it's not in the middle of your garden; it's in the middle of your daddy's vegetable garden.'

Both boys just laughed; it was such a relief to Harry as he so wanted to help his mummy and daddy and help Ethelred go back to see his parents as well.

'Get a spade and dig over there,' pointed Ethelred to a patch in the vegetable garden that Mr Alliss had already started to dig. 'It won't take long as your daddy almost found it by accident the other day when he was working in the garden; he's dug quite a big hole already.'

Harry opened the gate into the vegetable garden; it didn't give him any problems opening it and started digging. It was hard work, but he was determined to help his friend and his mummy and daddy.

"Crash!" Suddenly, Harry's spade hit something very solid.

'Well done, Harry, I think you've found it! Get your daddy,' said a very excited Ethelred, 'it will be heavy and your daddy is stronger than you.'

'My daddy has gone to work, perhaps Mummy might be able to help,' said Harry.

'I don't think so, it's very heavy,' Ethelred replied. Harry didn't really have much of a choice, so he ran into the house and then much to his surprise found that his daddy had come back from work and was sitting having a cup of tea in the kitchen. Mr Alliss stood up and lifted Harry up giving him a big hug. 'What are you doing, Harry?' he asked.

'I thought you were at work, Daddy,' said Harry.

'Yes, I know, but things didn't work out in the office, so I came home instead,' said Mr Alliss, a little bit downbeat.

'Daddy, Daddy, you've got to come quick, no, no, now come quickly.' And Harry tugged and pushed his daddy out of the kitchen and into the garden.

'All right, all right, Harry, I'll follow you, don't worry, what have you got to show me?' said Mr Alliss wondering what this was all about. But Harry was too excited to speak now, so he just ran to where the hole had been dug, then pointing to the hole Harry said, 'Look, Daddy, I found a treasure chest!'

Now Mr Alliss didn't understand what on earth was going on, but he did see a rusty lid that looked like the top of an old treasure chest. He jumped into the hole and started to heave at the chest. It was as Ethelred had said, it was rather heavy! Luckily, Harry managed to find Mr Keith who was in his garden at the same time and asked him to help. Between the two of them, they eventually managed to free the chest and drag it out of the hole.

Chapter Three – The Discovery

'Oh my,' said Mrs Alliss when they eventually managed to open the chest. There was this beautiful golden bracelet that looked almost like a snake being so smooth and slippery. It was so bright that it shone like a light in the kitchen. It was quite a find amongst the other gold cups and coins and even an old book. Mr Keith said that Mr Alliss would have to tell the people in the museum that he has found this treasure; he was sure it would be fine but that's Law. So, thanks to Harry and Ethelred, the Alliss's house was now safe.

'Well done, Harry!'

Mrs Alliss cried and cried after Mr Keith said what he thought this treasure would be worth. Grown-ups do that sometimes when they're happy. It seemed strange to Harry, but that's life Mr Keith explained.

It was a few days later after all the excitement had died down that Harry went back to his tree and sat on his bench. 'Ethelred, Ethelred,' called out Harry but Ethelred didn't appear. Then a little piece of paper floated down from the tree. Harry picked it up; there was some writing on it. Now Harry could read, but he wasn't sure of the writing as it seemed difficult to read as the writing was very old fashioned. Just then his mummy appeared and sat down next to her son.

'What are you doing, Harry?' asked Mrs Alliss.

Passing the piece of paper to his mummy, Harry asked, 'Can you please read this letter?' Mrs Alliss took the piece of paper, surprised that it looked so old and the writing old fashioned and read it out. It said…

Dear Harry, thank you for releasing me from this tree. It was so kind of you. I'm now with my mother and father. Please don't forget me. Your best friend, Ethelred.

Harry started to cry. 'Are you all right, Harry,' said Mrs Alliss, 'do you know who Ethelred is?'

'Yes, he was my best friend,' said Harry. Now Mrs Alliss knew that when Harry cries and says that there's nothing wrong then there is something wrong, so she gave him a hug; she was sure that he will tell her later, but not now.

'Bye, Ethelred,' said Harry.

'Bye, Ethelred,' said Mrs Alliss, 'and thank you so, so much.'

P.S. The people in the museum agreed what the jewels were worth, and as they were found on Mr and Mrs Alliss's property, they could keep it. The jewels were sold and Mr Alliss paid off the mortgage. The Alliss family were saved. Thank you, Ethelred.

Book Two

Harry and the New Puppy

Chapter One – Who Wants a Dog?

Harry woke up as normal, got dressed and went downstairs for his breakfast. Mr Alliss had already gone to work and his brother Hugo was still getting ready so Harry was on his own with his mummy in the kitchen.

'What would you like for breakfast, Harry…cereal?' asked Mrs Alliss.

'Mmmmm, I was thinking, Mummy,' replied Harry. *Oh*, thought Mrs Alliss, *what can this be about…?*

'Mummy, can we have a dog? I know that Daddy would like a dog, and it would be so much fun,' Harry asked.

'They need a lot of care, Harry, walkies and grooming and looking after them, it's a lot of responsibility,' Mrs Alliss reminded Harry.

'I know, Mummy, but I will look after it and so will Hugo; he'd like a dog as well,' said Harry to support his case for a dog.

'So, you have already asked Hugo about this dog then, Harry?' quizzed Mrs Alliss.

'Oh, yes, Mummy, we had a chat about it,' said Harry.

'When was that exactly…?' asked Mrs Alliss.

'Last night,' replied Harry.

'Hmmm…so not too long ago,' Mrs Alliss replied thoughtfully.

'Well, no, but I know Hugo would like a dog, and Daddy wants a dog…please, Mummy, please,' implored Harry.

'…and what sort of dog would you like, Harry, and of course, Hugo would need to say the same,' asked Mrs Alliss.

'Well, we think it should be a Labrador; it's such a friendly dog. Mr Riggley-Sey has got one and it's always wagging its tail and licking me,' said Harry.

'Well, have your breakfast first, Harry, and I will talk to Hugo, and Daddy of course when he comes back from work,' said Mrs Alliss.

'Promise?' Harry asked.

'Yes, of course, Harry, you needn't ask,' said Mrs Alliss.

Two weeks went by and Harry and Hugo were still asking if they could have a dog. Harry thought that getting his younger brother to ask as well will make it easier for their parents to agree, but then something happened and Harry went up to his daddy and said, 'Daddy, I don't want a Labrador or a puppy any more,' quickly followed by, 'nor does Hugo; we both want a dog from a dog's home.'

'Oh,' said Mr Alliss, 'now that's a bit of surprise, Harry, I didn't think you even knew about dog homes.'

'I watched…I mean we watched a program on TV about abandoned dogs,' said Harry 'and it's so sad that they are not cared for by anyone anymore.'

'Very true, Harry, it's very sad the way some people look after their pets and then abandon them when they don't want them anymore. That's very good of you, Harry; I'm very proud of you to think like that,' said Mr Alliss.

'…and Hugo,' Harry replied quickly.

'Oh, yes, of course, and Hugo as well,' replied Mr Alliss.

So, Mr Alliss went onto his computer and started to search for local dogs' homes and how to adopt a dog. After a while and a few phone calls later, Mr Alliss called out to the boys.

'Right, Harry, Hugo, I have found a dog's home which we can go to tomorrow. We will all go and hopefully find a dog that you, I mean, we all like,' said Mr Alliss. Harry jumped for joy.

'Oh, thank you, Daddy,' he said, 'I will be, I mean, we will be the best dog looker afters ever!'

'I know you will,' said Mrs Alliss who was listening to their little chat. 'I know you will, Harry…'

Chapter Two – Finding a Dog to Love

It was Sunday morning when Mr Alliss and the boys drove to the local dog's home. It was a longish drive, but that was all right as Harry and Hugo were both quite excited with the prospect of finding a dog to adopt. When they eventually arrived, they went straight into the kennel's office and asked about any dogs that they might be able to give a home to.

'And whose dog is this going to be?' asked the dogs homes carer.

'Mine, I mean ours,' said Harry pointing to Hugo and himself.

Dolly Pinkerton smiled, she was the dog's home owner and has many times seen the excitement that young children have when they are given a dog, but when she looked at Harry, she knew instinctively that this little boy will really care for and look after his dog.

'Right, Harry, the secret of looking for a dog is not to look for it at all, but to let the dog find you. Dogs aren't like humans; they have a sixth sense about people. People don't have that anymore, so a dog will immediately know exactly who they like and who they trust.' Dolly Pinkerton took Harry by his hand and led him towards the kennels. There were many dogs in the kennels. Some barked at Harry, others didn't even look up at him and others were very shy and didn't want to come towards Harry when he looked at them through the kennel's wire gates.

You have to remember, Harry, that these dogs have been abandoned by their owners; they are all very frightened and very sad; they have had a bad experience so you have to expect to be a bit disappointed at times when looking for a rescued dog,' said Dolly.

'But they don't like me,' said Harry sounding a bit upset.

'No, don't worry, Harry, the right dog is always just around the corner; it just takes a little bit of time to find the right one,' consoled Dolly.

They walked a little bit further along, but none of the dogs seemed to be very friendly and Harry was starting to look very upset. He hadn't expected this to happen; he thought it would be a happy time, but it turned out to be the complete opposite!

'Well, not to worry,' said Dolly, 'perhaps if you come back in a few weeks' time there may be a dog that you like and they like you, is that okay, Harry...?' said Dolly trying hard to cheer Harry up.

Just at that precise moment, Hugo turned around to Mrs Dolly Pinkerton and asked, 'Is there a dog in that kennel over there that we can see.' Hugo was pointing at a kennel that was a bit hidden away from the rest of the other kennels.

'Oh, I forgot about that kennel, that's where we keep a dog that is ready to go to new home,' Dolly said. 'I think the dog that was in there has already been taken away earlier, but I'll check.'

'Barbara, Barbara,' shouted Dolly, and out of the office, an old lady came out.

'Yes, Mrs Pinkerton,' said Barbara in a low voice.

'Is the dog in Kennel K9 taken now?'

'No, Mrs Pinkerton, the people who said they wanted it changed their minds in the end, and they didn't come to collect it as planned,' said Barbara in her low voice.

'Typical,' said Dolly now sounding a little bit cross. 'Well, Harry, let's look, you never know what's around the corner.'

Dolly walked on ahead, and when Harry reached the kennel, there was a little dog that immediately came up to Harry as he was standing outside by the kennel's gate.

'Oh, look, Harry, he really likes you,' said Dolly with a big smile on her face. 'Shall I get him out?'

'Oh, yes, please,' said Harry excitedly; could this be their new dog!

Harry and Hugo and the little dog all seemed to be very happy with each other. The boys patted and stroked him and the little dog was rolling around and licking both the boys. He was very excited, wagging his tiny little tail. It was a perfect match!

'Well, he definitely likes you boys,' said Dolly, 'always a very good sign.'

'What sort of breed is it?' asked Mr Alliss.

'Well, it's what we call in the trade a Fineze 57,' said Dolly, 'a Scottie terrier mix, slightly larger than a terrier but still a nice size for a family dog. He's very friendly and certainly likes your boys.'

'Yes, I can see that…and how old is it?' Mr Alliss enquired further.

'We can't be exact as I'm sure, you understand, but we think he's about a year old. He's house trained if that's what you mean as well,' said Dolly.

'Well, boys, if you're happy, we'll take the little pooch home with us,' said Mr Alliss.

'Oh, yes, please, Daddy,' they both replied. Harry was so, so happy, as was Hugo.

'What name will you give it?' asked Dolly.

'Pluto,' said Harry immediately.

'Pluto it is,' said Dolly, 'it's a great name, I think you will all be very happy together.'

Mr Alliss went over into the dog kennel's office and paid for Pluto. It wasn't very much money, more of a donation more than anything else. He also got a dog lead and collar, a feeding bowl, some dog food and of course the strict feeding instructions from Mrs Pinkerton. They all thanked Dolly for her care and attention in finding them a dog, then they all got back into the family car and drove home. Harry was happy with his new friend.

It was later during the first week of having Pluto in the home that Mr Alliss remarked to Mrs Alliss after the boys had gone to bed. 'Well, I must admit little Pluto is a very nice little dog. I was a bit worried at first, but he's nice and easy to live with. Doesn't make any mess, doesn't yap like some dogs do and really likes playing football with the boys. I think I picked a winner,' he said.

Mrs Alliss just smiled. 'Well done, darling, I knew you would,' she said.

In fact, Pluto loved playing football with the boys. Harry would often say that Pluto is just too good as he always gets the ball and then the boys find it difficult to get the ball back!

Chapter Three - The Fair

It was coming up to the weekend of the fair. Harry and Hugo were going to take Pluto for a walk. They would often walk with their neighbour Mr Keith. Mr Keith loved dogs even though he didn't have one himself, but he was very happy to go for a walk with Pluto and the boys. The boys walked towards the park where the fair was going to take place. The fair ground owners were putting the fair and the rides together; there was a lot of commotion going on. Harry and Hugo were walking on ahead with Pluto with Mr Keith following when suddenly a large group of people appeared almost from nowhere.

Mr Keith shouted out to the boys, 'Now stay together, boys, don't wander off.' But in the crowd, the boys were swallowed up and unfortunately Mr Keith lost sight of them.

The boys looked around, but they couldn't see Mr Keith and started to walk around the fair completely lost. They eventually stumbled onto a road in which was parked a van and another car. Harry looked and could see that two men were trying to get something from this car and they appeared to be up to no good. The car's driver was struggling to protect himself whilst the two men were trying to steal something from him.

'STOP!' shouted Harry. It was a brave thing to do, but then Harry remembered what WPC Hillary Evans had said to him, "Call the police first." But it was too late!

One of the men looked up and said, 'Get them, Jake, they've seen us now, throw them into the van.' Both men caught up with the boys and Harry and Hugo were bundled into their van, with Pluto running off into the woods.

Both boys were trapped inside the van. It was a bit dark and smelly and they were very scared. 'I thought that Pluto would protect us,' said Hugo.

'So did I,' said Harry feeling very scared and wishing that he hadn't said anything about the robbery. They both huddled up to each other frightened of what was going to happen to them next. The van drove for a while, then it stopped and the doors were swung open. The men took hold of both Harry and Hugo and roughly threw them into an old rundown shed.

'We'll sort them out later,' one of the villains said, with an evil laugh.
'I'm scared, Harry,' said Hugo.
'Me too,' said Harry feeling his knees tremble a bit.
'Will anyone save us?' said Hugo. Harry closed his eyes and prayed like he never prayed before.
'I wish Aunty Dare was here,' said Hugo. 'She would rescue us.'
'Yes,' said Harry; he really didn't know what more to say to his little brother, but he tried to be as brave as he could.

Chapter Four – Pluto to the Rescue

Harry was pretty sure that it had become quite late now as the light was fading through the cracks in the walls that were in the shed. They didn't have any food and were very thirsty as well. Hugo kept crying and calling for his mummy and Harry would huddle him and say that everything would be all right, but he really wasn't sure it would be. Then suddenly, Harry heard a noise. 'Shhhh, Hugo, quiet…what's that noise, where's it coming from?' It was like a scrapping noise and then the ground where they were both sitting just fell away to reveal a hole.

'What's happening?' asked Hugo, becoming more and more frightened. Then out of the hole popped Pluto, jumping up and licking both boys.

'Pluto's found us! Pluto's found us!' they both yelled with absolute joy hugging the little dog, who was so pleased to see them too.

'Quietly, boys…' said a voice from somewhere. Harry put his ear to the entrance to the tunnel that Pluto had dug and he could hear that it was Aunty Dare. 'Quickly now, boys, go through the tunnel, I'm waiting on the other side for you.'

Harry took hold of Hugo and said, 'You go first, and don't stop till you get to Aunty Dare.'

The tunnel wasn't very wide and both boys had to use all their strength to climb through it, but Aunty Dare reached out and helped to pull out Hugo and then Harry. Little Pluto came out last, looking very pleased with himself.

'Aunty, how did you…'

'Shh, Harry, no time for any chitchat, follow that path down to the little lane. Mr Keith will be there in his car smoking his pipe. Knock on his window and he'll drive you to safety,' instructed Aunty Dare. 'Pluto' – Aunty Dare took hold of Pluto and held him by his head – 'you lead the boys to Mr Keith; now go quick as quick.'

The boys looked at each other and followed Pluto who kept just ahead of them so that they could see him in the darkness. After walking for a short while in the darkness, Harry exclaimed, 'There, Hugo, look, it's Mr Keith and he's sitting in the car smoking his pipe just as Aunty Dare had told us he would.' The boys ran down towards Mr Keith's car and knocked on his driver's door window.

Opening the window, Mr Keith said, 'Quickly, boys, get into the back and hide under the blanket.' The boys jumped into the back with Pluto following them. Once inside, they put the blanket over themselves, and holding onto Pluto, Harry said, 'Ready, Mr Keith.'

The car slowly moved off and Harry thought that it was strange that it wasn't making any noise from the engine. Mr Keith hadn't even put his lights on, the car was just rolling down the hill. Then Harry looked again. In the darkness, he could see that Aunty Dare was sitting on the bonnet of the car and it looked like she was giving Mr Keith directions to go left or right or straight ahead, but how was that possible!

Eventually, after they had gone down the hill, Mr Keith spoke. 'Okay, boys, we're are clear of the robbers now; they can't see or hear the car so it's safe for me to put the engine and lights on. I'll drive on now. Just around the bend is a police car, we'll be safe then.'

'Where's Aunty Dare gone?' asked Harry.

'Aunty Dare, where was she?' asked a very surprised Mr Keith.

'She was sitting on your bonnet, Mr Keith, giving you directions as you went down the hill in the darkness,' answered Harry.

'Really! Well, I didn't see her,' replied an even more confused Mr Keith.

'So how did you know how to go down the hill in the darkness, we couldn't see a thing!' asked an amazed Harry.

'I really don't know, boys; I really don't know at all. I don't know how you found me, why I was parked where I was parked or anything really, even about the police car. It's a complete mystery to me, but I just know what I know, but don't ask me why I know because I don't know!' said Mr Keith. Harry said nothing, he was just as confused as Mr Keith now!

Within a few minutes, Mr Keith had driven around the corner and there sure enough was a police car parked up. Police constables, Ben Johnson, PC No 666 and Rebecca Wade, WPC No 123, approached Mr Keith's car.

'Good evening, sir, do you mind telling us what you are doing driving at this time of night?' said PC Johnson.

But before Mr Keith could reply, and he was having a few problems trying to recall what had happened, WPC Wade called out, 'Don't worry, Ben' – because WPC Wade had looked through the back door window of Mr Keith's car and seen the boys – 'these are the boys we are looking for.'

Opening the rear door, WPC Wade asked, 'Are you all right, boys?'

'Yes,' said a very happy Harry, '…and Mr Keith rescued us.'

'…and Pluto!' shouted out Hugo.

'All right then, let's have a look at you both, well, you're a bit dirty, but considering everything you both have gone through, you aren't too bad. Would you like a drink and a piece of chocolate?' said WPC Wade.

'Oh, yes, please,' said the boys together. WPC Wade reached into her top pocket and brought out a bar of chocolate and gave it to the boys. That was greeted with two big smiles from two very grateful little boys!

'Don't worry, the hot chocolate will come later but have this bottle of water as a drink,' said WPC Wade.

'Thank you very much, miss,' the boys said together.

Chapter Five – The Round Up

'ALL RIGHT, ALL RIGHT this is the MIS,' said a voice from somewhere. 'I'm taking charge now.'

'You, get some back up, and you get an ambulance, and be double quick,' said the voice to the two police constables.

'Yes, ma'am,' they replied together without any protest, and out from the shadows appeared Aunty Dare.

'Aunty Dare, Aunty Dare…!' called out an overjoyed Harry at seeing his aunty again.

'You know Aunty Dare?' whispered WPC Wade. 'Gosh, she's a VIP in these circles. Counter terrorism and serious crime, you name it, she's involved; you don't mess with her!'

'She's our aunty,' said Hugo. 'She's so much fun.'

WPC Wade just rolled her eyes and quickly got on with her business, all she could say was, 'Mmm.' Soon two van loads of policemen drove past.

'Those robbers have had it now,' said PC Johnson, 'they'll be eating porridge soon.' Then the ambulance arrived and the boys were taken inside the ambulance to be checked over by the paramedics.

'What about Pluto?' asked Harry.

'Now don't worry, Harry,' said Aunty Dare, 'I'll take care of Pluto; he's fine with me.'

'Here, boy,' she said, and Pluto almost jumped into her arms. 'No problem, boys, you'll see Pluto when you get home. Your mummy and daddy will be waiting for you at the hospital. Now don't stand there please, driver,' said Aunty Dare to the paramedic, 'quick as quick if you please.'

The ambulance and police car drove off into the night with Mr Keith following on behind still none the wiser from the events that had happened. In the inky darkness, Aunty Dare and Pluto were now standing alone.

'Well done, Dare, another case solved. I bet the men folk in the office will be very pleased with your exceptional clear up rate,' said Lady Vix appearing out of nowhere.

'Oh, Vix, you gave me quite a surprise sneaking up on me like that! Yes, I'm sure they will…' replied Aunty Dare with a long sigh.

Harry and the Little Boat

Chapter One – The Breakthrough

'Wake up, Harry, wake up it's time to go to swimming classes,' called out Mr Alliss. Harry threw his duvet over his head. *Oh no, not again*, Harry thought to himself.

'Come on, Hugo, you too, swimming classes, come on, boys.' Mr Alliss was in full reveille mode, calling out to the boys to hurry up and get dressed. Harry looked at his digital alarm clock. It said six o'clock in the morning! *That's so early*, he thought to himself, *if only Hugo could learn to swim a little bit quicker, we wouldn't have to get up so early on a Saturday morning.*

It wasn't long before both boys met downstairs with all their swimming kit in their little bags, all prepared the night before by Mrs Alliss. 'Come on, boys, let's get into the car and go to the swimming pool. Mr Attcliffe will be waiting for us,' said Mr Alliss. 'We all have to learn how to swim otherwise we will not be able to go on holiday to the Lakes and hire any boats to go out sailing.'

'We can all wear lifejackets, Daddy,' said Harry helpfully. Mr Alliss smiled to himself, he thought that was a very reasonable reply.

'Well done, Harry, that is a very good thing to do, but knowing how to swim will save you if we should ever get into difficulties…not that we ever will,' he added so as not to worry his boys.

'Hugo,' Harry said looking at his brother, 'you must hurry up and learn how to swim. My class isn't till nine o'clock so I have a very long wait now and no breakfast either until I finish my class!' Now Hugo wanted to learn to swim, but he wasn't a natural in the water. Harry had taken to it like a duck to water and was now in the intermediate class, but Hugo struggled. Harry wanted to help but he didn't know how to.

'A big A for effort today, Hugo, it will mean a lot if you can learn to float properly, the rest will then come very quickly,' said Mr Alliss.

'I'll try and do my best, Daddy,' said Hugo but lacking any conviction. It was proving very hard for him to learn to swim no matter how hard he tried.

'I know you will, Hugo, we'll be cheering you on,' said Mr Alliss. When they arrived at the swimming pool, the boys went into the boys changing room and Hugo got ready. Harry put his swimming kit in a locker but stayed as he was for he still had a long time to wait.

'Good luck, Hugo,' said Harry, 'you'll do it, I know you will.' That meant a lot to Hugo, as he didn't want to disappoint his brother or his daddy. He made his way to the pool; Mr Attcliffe was waiting by the poolside.

'Hello, Hugo, ready to start the lesson?'

'Yes, Mr Attcliffe,' said Hugo feeling a bit nervous. Now Mr Attcliffe was a large but friendly man. He has taught swimming to lots of children across many, many years, but Hugo was now becoming a bit of a challenge for him, even with having so much experience teaching children to swim. But Mr Attcliffe was never going to give up. He liked Hugo, he just needed to get over his nervousness in the water and then he would be fine, he thought to himself.

'Okay, Hugo, take this float and hold it out, then push hard against the poolside wall and see how far you will go. Just relax, Hugo, don't be nervous, there's nothing to be nervous about, I'm here to catch you,' said Mr Attcliffe.

The water in the pool was quite shallow, and it was quite warm today, warmer than it usually was in fact, because sometimes it was downright freezing thought Hugo, but today, it was nice. Hugo thought hard, he didn't want to disappoint anybody, so being as positive as he could be he pushed as hard as he could away from the poolside wall as he was told to do. He held the float straight and true in front of him and somehow he wasn't sinking like he normally does!

'WELL DONE, HUGO,' bellowed Mr Attcliffe. In fact, it was so loud that all the children in the pool turned around and started to clap for Hugo. Hugo looked back over the distance that he had just floated and was so pleased with himself, he made it at last!

'I think you've turned a corner, young man,' said Mr Attcliffe, 'that was outstanding, well done, Hugo, well done! Now let's do it again, and let's see if you can reach the other end of the pool, just paddle with your legs like I showed you.'

With renewed confidence, Hugo went back to the poolside wall and looked up to see if Harry and his daddy were watching him. Sure enough, they were, with big smiles on their faces. That really cheered Hugo up. Then he caught sight of Aunty Dare, or at least he thought that he caught sight of Aunty Dare and she was also waving to him. He blinked to get the water out from his eyes, and Aunty Dare just slowly disappeared but still waving all at the same time. How strange he thought, did he really see that!

Hugo gave a big push away from the poolside wall and paddled with his legs as Mr Attcliffe had shown him and glided gently to the other side of the pool. That was the big breakthrough that everyone was waiting for. Mr Attcliffe was beside himself; he kept telling Hugo how brilliantly he was doing and Harry and Mr Alliss kept waving and cheering from the viewing deck. It really made Hugo's morning. Hugo was so, so happy.

Chapter Two – Mr Riggley-Sey

'Well, boys, that was an excellent day today,' said Mr Alliss. 'As a treat, Hugo, you can have anything you want for breakfast, just say it and I'll cook it.' Now Mr Alliss was a good cook, but Harry liked his mummy's cooking best because she made lovely cakes, but Mr Alliss was still quite good as well. His Coq au Vin was a legend in the Alliss family!

'Can we have a full English breakfast, Daddy?' asked Harry cheekily.

'It isn't your choice, Harry,' said Mr Alliss, 'it's Hugo's and only Hugo's to choose, now what would you like, Hugo?'

'I think I would like toast and jam, and bacon, and some sausages with scrambled eggs,' said Hugo. Mr Alliss smiled to himself.

'Hmmm, looks like you got what you wanted, Harry. No problem, Hugo, your wish is my command.' And they all loudly cheered; it was a great morning!

After a few weeks, Hugo's swimming just got better and better. In fact, he moved up a class and so the boys didn't have to start till eight o'clock in the morning. Harry could have a little sleep-in on a Saturday morning and that made him very happy.

It was after one of the swimming lessons was over and they were all going home that Mr Alliss said, 'Harry, Hugo, I'm really pleased with your swimming progress, so I have booked a little holiday in the Lakes for all of us. We will have a chalet by the side of the lake and we can now hire a little boat to go sailing in. We cannot go sailing without lifejackets, but we all know that already, don't we?' Harry and Hugo both nodded.

'When will we be going?' asked Harry.

'In a few weeks' time when the weather warms up hopefully,' said Mr Alliss.

Now Harry knew that one of his neighbours had a boat which he would often take to the Lakes. So, Harry decided that it would be good to see him because he only lived two doors away and was a nice man. Mr Alan Riggley-Sey was an ex-naval captain and loved everything connected with the water and sailing. He would quite often go and see Mr Keith, who was Harry's other neighbour and they would chat away about boats and such things. So, after breakfast when they had come back from another swimming lesson, Harry asked if he could go and knock on Mr Riggley-Sey's house and ask if he could have a look at his boat.

'Yes, I think that will be fine, Harry,' said Mr Alliss, 'actually, I saw him talking to Mr Keith, so I'll take you over now if you like.' And with that, they both went over to see Mr Riggley-Sey.

'Hello, there, young man,' said Mr Riggley-Sey to Harry, 'what brings you here?'

'I'd like to see your boat,' said Harry excitedly.

'Yes, of course, I will be delighted to show you, but it's a motor cruiser, there is a difference,' said Mr Riggley-Sey, 'but you are more than welcome; come this way.' They both walked into the large garage where the motor cruiser was kept. It was sitting on a trailer so that it could be towed when Mr Riggley-Sey went to the Lakes. Harry noticed the name on the bow of the boat, but he had trouble pronouncing it.

'She A Po Taj,' said Mr Riggley-Sey.

'Shia Potage,' said Harry.

'Yes, absolutely,' said Mr Riggley-Sey, 'well done, Harry, that's spot on. Don't ask me how I got that name; it just popped into my head one day and just stuck,' he said with a big smile on his face.

'We are going to the Lakes soon,' said Harry, 'now that we can all swim, Daddy says that it's safe for us to go.'

'Absolutely,' Mr Riggley-Sey replied, 'your daddy is spot on; I always think that you mustn't play in the water if you don't know how to swim; the water can be quite dangerous especially if you don't respect it. Well, I look forward to seeing you on the Lakes, Harry, and I'll take you out on my motor cruiser. It will be fun; you'll see it better when it's on the water rather than here sitting on this trailer.' Harry was very pleased that he had gone to see Mr Riggley-Sey so he gave him his hand to shake hands with him. Mr Riggley-Sey was so impressed with Harry for doing that. Grasping his little hand, he said, 'You're more than welcome, Harry, bring your family and we can all go out, there's plenty of room aboard; it will be great fun.'

Chapter Three – The Holiday Drama

The time had come for the Alliss family to pack their suitcases and get ready to go to the Lakes. It was decided that Pluto would stay with Mr Keith, as he really liked walking Pluto and it was a lot better than putting Pluto into kennels. Harry would miss Pluto, but he knew that he would be all right with Mr Keith.

They were all very excited about the mini holiday and Harry knew that Mr Riggley-Sey was there already with his motor cruiser. 'Will we see Mr Riggley-Sey?' asked Harry.

'Yes, of course, he said for us to visit him,' Mr Alliss replied. It was going to be fun going in a motor cruiser thought Harry because Mr Keith had already told him that it was a fast cruiser. It took a while to drive to the Lakes; it was further than Harry had imagined. Mr Alliss did most of the driving although Mrs Alliss did a bit of the driving as well. Harry thought that both his parents were good drivers although his mummy sometimes did have a few problems parking in tight spots. Harry thought that he'd be a very good driver when he grows up.

It was the second day of their holiday. Mrs Alliss stayed in the chalet to tidy up. The boys and Mr Alliss were walking along the jetty looking at all the pleasure boats which were moored up, which could be hired out to go onto the water. It appeared to Harry that all you needed was a yellow ticket with a number on it, which you gave to the jetty boat boy who was managing the boats and then away you went. So, Mr Alliss went over to the hire shop to buy the ticket. When he got back, he said to Harry, 'Here, Harry, take this ticket, I've got to pop over to the gift shop to get a few things and I'll meet you by the boat.' What could possibly go wrong!

The boys went towards the jetty boat boy and gave him the ticket. The boy murmured something under his breath which Harry didn't understand and told the boys to follow him. He led them to the boat, told them to get in, which they did, then he started the outboard engine and pushed them off.

Harry looked at Hugo and they both realised that the boat was moving forward and nobody was steering it, also their daddy wasn't there either. Why did the jetty boy do that! The boat just got faster and faster and the boys were starting to get a bit worried if something bad was going to happen. Harry ran to the back of the boat and took hold of the rudder which steered the boat, but it didn't move! The lever which controlled the speed of the boat also felt jammed so Harry couldn't slow the boat down. It just continued going faster and faster, in fact the front of the boat was now lifting above the water showing that this boat was going much too fast.

'HELP!' shouted Hugo. 'HELP US!'

Both boys were getting very frightened, because the jetty boat boy had not even given them a chance to put on their lifejackets, and they didn't even know where they were in any case! Then Harry saw a sign written in red, "DANGER – WEIR AHEAD – TURN BACK".

Harry knew that they were now in terrible danger. What to do, what to do, he wished that Aunty Dare was here, she would know what to do. Then suddenly on his right, he saw a familiar motor cruiser. Harry recognised the craft, it was Mr Riggley-Sey in the Shia Potage!

'Quick, Hugo,' Harry shouted, 'look, Mr Riggley-Sey, wave like mad to him.'

Both boys stood up and frantically waved, shouting at the top of their voices,' HELP, HELP US, HELP…'

Then as if by magic, they saw the motor cruiser lift its bow, and with a huge plume of water coming from the back of the boat, it sped like a rocket towards where the boys were. It was an amazing sight to see even though they were now in great danger. Mr Riggley-Sey had seen the little boat and he was going to save them no matter what. He pushed his cruiser to its absolute maximum and beyond, nothing was spared! Very soon, the cruiser drew alongside the boys' boat maintaining the same speed as the little craft. There were only moments left before there would be a big accident.

'Quick, Harry, grab this rope and tie it to your boat!' Mr Riggley-Sey shouted. Harry caught the rope and tied it to his little boat. Gently, Mr Riggley-Sey used his motor cruiser to steer both boats away from the weir. They all could hear the crashing of the water as it tumbled over the weir; it was a desperately scary sound!

'Harry, push that lever backwards, it will shut the engine off!' shouted Mr Riggley-Sey. Both boys pushed as hard as they could, and slowly, the lever gave way going back till they felt it going CLICK, and at last, the engine stopped!

'Well done, boys, you've saved the day,' said Mr Riggley-Sey, really delighted that he was able to save the boys from what would have been a terrible accident. Once safely away from the weir, he stopped his motor cruiser and jumped on board the boys' boat. They were both badly shaken by what had just happened and just thanked him for saving them.

'No, well done to you boys, you did well, very well indeed. You kept your heads and that saved the day. You should never have been allowed to go out like you did and with no lifejackets on either. I'll speak to the jetty master; this must never happen again,' said Mr Riggley-Sey, who was now getting very cross because he knew this should have never happened but not with the boys; it really wasn't their fault.

'Your motor cruiser is very fast, Mr Riggley-Sey,' said Harry. Hugo nodded in agreement; he had been amazed how quickly it reached them.

'Yes, I must admit it went a lot faster today than it has ever done before. It was like there was this huge hand pushing me towards you boys; I've never experienced anything like it,' said Mr Riggley-Sey, 'but a good job too.' Harry could only think of one thing to explain that… "Aunty Dare", but he said nothing, just smiled and said "Thank you, Aunty" very quietly under his breath.

Mr Riggley-Sey got both boys on board his boat and then made sure that the hire boat was properly tied up to his motor cruiser so that he could tow it back to the jetty. There were lots of people standing by the jetty all pointing to them when they arrived. They had all seen what had happened. The boat boy on the jetty was looking very sheepish; he knew that he was now in big, big trouble.

Mr Alliss was also on the jetty having seen what had happened; he ran up to where Mr Riggley-Sey moored up and thanked him for saving his boys. He gave Harry and Hugo the biggest hug ever; he was quite overcome really, but Mr Riggley-Sey said that both boys were just wonderful for not losing their heads and keeping calm. He was very proud of them both. Mr Alliss was bursting with pride for his brave boys. The jetty master then came up and apologised for what had happened. He said that he would sack the jetty boy for allowing the craft to leave without a responsible adult, but then Harry said, 'No, don't let him lose his job; he made a bad mistake, but he won't make it again.' All the adults were amazed by what Harry had just said and stood back in total silence waiting for someone to speak.

'Well, I'm very impressed with your young son, Mr Alliss; he's wise beyond his years,' said the jetty master. Turning to the jetty boy, he said, 'Ryan, you owe a big SORRY to these young lads for what you did. I don't understand why you did what you did, but it could have turned out nasty, and you know that! You owe a big THANK YOU to young Harry for saving your job, because quite honestly, you deserve to be sacked. Make no mistake. I would have sacked on the spot had it not been for young Harry!'

Chapter Four – All's Well

'That was quite amazing what you boys did today. To say that I'm proud to know you and have you as my neighbours is an honour, young Harry and Hugo. My boat is your boat. I'll show you how to cruise in it, providing of course that your daddy will let me,' said Mr Riggley-Sey. Mr Alliss could only nod his head; it had been such a frightening thing for him to witness, he was just so happy that his boys were safe. It was a lesson learnt for everyone.

Well, what a day and what a week the Allisses had cruising up and down the Lakes in the Shia Potage. How that motor cruiser travelled over the water was fantastic; it was so smooth and powerful. Mr Riggley-Sey would let both boys steer the craft so that they understood the controls; it was great fun. It also had a nice cabin where they could have something to eat and drink when they stopped to take in the sights and sounds around the Lakes. Everyone had so much fun. But Harry knew that it was really Aunty Dare who somehow saved them on that awful day; she was always looking after him like a guardian angel and that made him feel very safe…

Harry and Santa Claus

Chapter One – The Christmas Turkey

It was Christmas Eve and the big day was fast approaching. Both Harry and Hugo were getting very excited about Santa coming. Both boys believed in Santa Claus, and let's face it, who doesn't! They helped their mummy to decorate the house putting up the Christmas tree, hanging up the paper chains and glass boules and placing out the Christmas cards that had been received by the family. Harry had decorated the fireplace in the front room ready for Santa to come down the chimney. He even asked his daddy whether the chimney had been swept, as he didn't want Santa to get stuck in it. Very thoughtful thought Mr and Mrs Alliss, but so typical of Harry! Pluto the dog very wisely took the opportunity to rest up in his basket in the kitchen, away from the toing and froing of all the Christmas preparation and decoration activity. Chewing on his bone was far preferable; it was after all very good for a dog's teeth!

Mrs Alliss then asked Mr Alliss to collect the Christmas turkey from the butcher's where it had been ordered. 'Boys, do you want to come with me and get the turkey?' Mr Alliss called out. Hugo was busy making mince pies in the kitchen with Mrs Alliss so he couldn't go, but Harry was free so he went to the shop. Mr Alliss drove down to their local butcher's shop, which wasn't very far away. They were both singing Christmas carols and were in very jolly spirits when they arrived at the butcher's shop.

On entering the shop, they were greeted by Mr Carver the butcher, who looked very downbeat with a very long face. 'Oh, Mr Alliss, I have some terrible news for you. Last night, my stock room was burgled and all my customers' turkeys were stolen. It's a complete disaster, as I cannot find another butcher who can supply me with anymore turkeys. I tried to ring you earlier, but I couldn't get through. I'm so, so terribly sorry, I can't apologise enough,' Mr Carver said.

Harry looked at his daddy and the look on his face told him that this was the worst news ever! There wasn't much more that could be said, so after picking up some sausages and some sliced ham, which was all that was left from the pilfered stock, Mr Alliss paid up, and with a heavy heart, they left for home. 'Oh dear, Harry, your mummy is going to be so upset when we tell her about the turkey,' said Mr Alliss.

'Is there any other shop we can go to?' asked Harry.

'No, Harry, I'm afraid not; we were warned that this year turkeys were going to be in very short supply, which I suppose is why the robbery took place. It's not just us, Harry, other people will have their Christmas ruined as well,' said Mr Alliss. They both got into the car and started the drive back home in silence; they were both very upset.

When Mr Alliss told Mrs Alliss of what had happened, Harry could see how upset his mummy was. He tried to give her a cuddle to try and cheer her up, but he became upset himself when he saw his mummy cry. 'I really don't know what I'll do to feed everyone over Christmas,' she said and walked back to the kitchen and sat down by the kitchen table. Harry went over to his mummy and she hugged him and ruffled his hair. 'We need all your magic now, Harry,' she said, 'we'll have to use what's in the freezer, I suppose, but it won't be the same. Still at least we do have some food in the house. I feel upset for those people who have very little or nothing to fall back on; we must never forget that, Harry.'

Chapter Two – Santa Arrives

After that awful news, the boys helped with the Christmas preparations as best as they could. Harry liked helping making the cakes and desserts, and Hugo loved making mince pies and other savouries. Mr Alliss did manage to get a piece of beef when Mr Carver phoned to tell them that he found some at the back of his storeroom. The robbers must have overlooked that part of the storeroom thankfully, he told them. So at least, the family would have something fresh rather than frozen for their Christmas dinner. It had been a very eventful and tiring day and the family decided to go to bed early ready for the big day tomorrow. They left the Christmas lights on for Santa, and the Christmas tree looked lovely as it glowed in dark.

Harry was fast asleep when something woke him during the night. He thought that perhaps it was Pluto, but as usual, Pluto was fast asleep at the foot of Harry's bed where he normally slept during the night. Harry looked at his digital clock, it said 00.00 Midnight. So quietly, he tippy toed downstairs wondering if it was Santa coming down the chimney. Perhaps he might surprise him and have a chat with him. Slowly, he opened the front room's door, and there in the glow of the Christmas tree lights, he saw the familiar shape of Father Christmas. Santa had already come down the chimney!

'Hello, Santa,' Harry said excitedly.

'Shhhh,' Santa replied, putting his finger to his lips, 'we must be very quiet, we don't want to wake everyone up. Come in, Harry, and close the door,' Santa whispered.

'How did you know it's me?' asked Harry.

'Well, I know a lot about you, Harry. I have my ways of knowing about the children I visit, and I knew that you would come down and see me as well,' Santa said.

'How did you know that? I only woke up by accident,' said Harry, 'and thought I would come downstairs just in case it was you.'

'Ah, you see, there is nothing accidental that happens at Christmas, Harry, everything happens for a reason, and there is a reason for everything happening,' said Santa. Harry thought about that for a minute or so then said, 'May I ask you a question, Santa, please?'

'Of course, you can, what is your question, Harry?' replied Santa. He always knew that children had lots of questions for him at Christmas time. It was part of his job!

'How do you manage to go to all the children's homes and deliver all of their presents over Christmas night, you don't have a very long time to do that and there are so many children to see,' asked Harry.

'Hmmm, that's a very, very, good question,' said Santa, 'and it's not that easy to explain. I could say that it's the magic of Christmas, but I can see that you're a very clever boy, Harry, and would need a better explanation than that!'

Harry and Santa sat on the sofa, and Santa took his hat off. His long white hair flowed down to his shoulders, and with his white beard, he looked just like

Harry always thought that Santa would look like, if he ever met him of course. The real Santa that is, not the ones in the shops you must pay to see!

'Well, Harry, it's about controlling time. You live in what we would call "normal" time with your minutes and hours, and you know how long something takes if your mummy says to you, "Harry, be downstairs in five minutes," don't you, Harry?' Harry nodded; he knew exactly what that meant when his mummy called him and told him he's got five minutes!

'Now Santa's time doesn't work exactly like that; we must work to a different clock, so as I give out all the presents to all the children I'm working normally like I am now with you, Harry, but your time is slowed down; it's almost frozen, so when you go back to bed, your time will have hardly moved, not even by a second. In that way, I can go around to hundreds of children with all their presents in less time than it's taken to talk to you now, Harry. Nobody will see me or hear me either! Check the time on your clock when you go back to your bed.' explained Santa, hoping that it all made sense to Harry. Santa knew that Harry was a clever little boy so he couldn't tell him any old story! Harry sat and nodded his head; it sorts of made sense. I mean Santa can only tell you the truth, after all!

'But I heard you, Santa,' said Harry.

'Ahh, yes, very good, Harry, good spot,' Santa said with a knowing smile.

'I know, but I deliberately made a noise that I wanted you to hear, Harry, as I wanted to give you this present in person,' he said.

'What is it?' asked Harry.

'No, it's not what is it, Harry, it's who is it for...' said Santa.

'Yes, I'm sorry, Santa,' said Harry looking and feeling a little bit embarrassed thinking that the present would have been for him.

'No, not to worry, Harry, I know you meant well, but this is for your brother Hugo, and I want you to tell Hugo that it's a very special present,' said Santa.

'Because it's from you, Santa?' Harry asked.

'Well, yes and no,' said Santa, 'but you will see that it will be a very useful present to you both, you'll see.'

'You must be very tired, Santa, with all the presents you have to deliver,' said Harry.

'Yes, it's a very hectic night all right, but I do a lot of training across the year to prepare for it,' said Santa with a wink. 'Now I must get on, and you must go back to bed, Harry. Have a very Happy and Merry Christmas to you and all your family, Harry,' said Santa.

'Thank you, Santa, and Happy Christmas to you; it was lovely meeting you.'

'Take care, Harry,' said Santa, and with that, Harry took the present for Hugo and left the front room leaving Santa to finish up putting out the other presents and went upstairs to go back into his bed. When he got to his room, he saw that Pluto was still fast asleep. Then Harry noticed that his alarm clock hadn't changed at all. It was still saying 00:00 Midnight and he must have spoken to Santa for at least ten minutes or maybe even longer! But as soon as Harry put his head on his pillow, he was fast asleep.

Chapter Three – An Amazing Day

It was Christmas Day and Harry woke up and made to go downstairs. Hugo was already outside his bedroom. 'Merry Christmas, Hugo,' said Harry.
'Merry Christmas, Harry,' said Hugo.

'I've got a present for you, Hugo. Santa gave it to me last night. He said that it was a very special present,' said Harry. Hugo went over to Harry thinking that his brother was telling him another one of his magical stories.

He took the present saying, 'Thank you, Harry,' and quickly unwrapped it. He was a bit surprised to find it was a torch!

Hugo switched on the torch and pointed it at Harry. The light from the torch bathed Harry in an incredible glow that covered him head to toe. Harry stood there shimmering in the light; it looked very magical. Hugo then passed the torch over to Harry and Harry shone the torch and pointed it at Hugo. Hugo was also bathed in light like Harry had been. He also looked so magical.

Wow, that's an amazing torch, Harry,' said Hugo, thinking that perhaps this wasn't just another one of Harry's magical stories, after all. 'Did Santa give it to you last night, did you see Santa then, Harry…?'

Harry nodded, but he didn't mention anything about his little chat with Santa, that would be hard to explain. 'Let's go downstairs.' So, Hugo popped the torch into his back pocket and followed Harry downstairs.

'Merry Christmas, Harry. Merry Christmas, Hugo,' said Mr Alliss waiting for them in the hallway.

'Merry Christmas, Daddy,' the boys said together.

'Did I hear that someone has got a torch for Christmas?' asked Mrs Alliss as she popped her head around from the kitchen.

'Yes,' said Hugo as he took the torch out of his back pocket and gave it to his mummy, 'You can use it, Mummy.' Mrs Alliss took the torch and walked back into the kitchen, with Hugo following. 'I was trying to find a jar of pickled gherkins that your daddy just loves, when the larder light suddenly went out,' explained Mrs Alliss.

Hugo was now expecting the larder to be bathed in light like he and Harry had been a few moments ago, but no! When Mrs Alliss turned the torch on, it just shone a beam of light like any ordinary torch would. Hugo was a bit surprised but didn't say anything.

'Found it!' said Mrs Alliss. Then looking at the torch, she remarked, 'This is a very nice torch, Hugo; did it come with batteries then?'

'Yes, Mummy,' said Hugo.

'Who gave it to you?' asked Mrs Alliss.

'Santa, Mummy,' replied Hugo.

'Yes, of course,' said Mrs Alliss, 'why did I even ask?'

'Surprisingly light for a torch with batteries,' said Mrs Alliss, but no matter, she handed the torch back to Hugo who then put it in his back pocket. They then started to make their way back to the front room to see Mr Alliss, Harry and Pluto of course and start the opening of the presents!

Now it is a tradition in the Alliss household that Mr Alliss is always the Christmas Elf, who gives out the presents. Harry doesn't mind as it makes his daddy happy and that makes everybody else happy as well.

'Shall I start?' said Mr Alliss kneeling by the Christmas tree reading the labels on the presents ready to give them out.

'This is for H—'

'STOP!' shouted Harry jumping up from the sofa where he was sitting with Hugo and his mummy. 'Its Aunty Dare and Lady Vix coming up the driveway.' And sure enough, they all heard the unmistakable "pop, pop, pop" sound of Aunty Dare's scooter.

Harry ran out of the house, even though he was still in his PJs followed by Hugo and Mrs Alliss. 'AUNTY DARE, LADY VIX!' Harry shouted excitedly. They all waited whilst Aunty Dare parked her scooter and then they gave each other a big hug.

'It's so good to see you, Aunty Dare and Lady Vix,' said Harry.

'We wouldn't miss it for the world, Harry,' Lady Vix replied.

It was at that point that Mrs Alliss, looking rather sad and forlorn, said, 'I'm so terribly sorry, Aunty Dare and Lady Vix, but we don't have a turkey for Christmas. There was a terrible robbery at the butcher's and our turkey was stolen. I was so upset last night that I forgot to call you to apologise.'

'Oh, don't worry, Nicola,' Lady Vix said going over to Mrs Alliss to give her a Christmas hug. 'Let's have a glass of bubbly to celebrate the day; I'm sure Dare will sort something out; she usually does.'

'Oh, I don't have any bubbly either,' said Mrs Alliss feeling that she was letting everyone down.

'Oh, please don't worry; let's both have a look; it's usually on the left-hand side of the fridge, let's go and have a look.' And with that, Lady Vix took Mrs Alliss by the arm and led her back to her kitchen.

'All right, Harry, now please take hold of my crash helmet as I must sort a few things out in my scooter's cubby hole.' Aunty Dare lifted the scooter's seat which hinged at the front to reveal a storage cubby hole. She started to rummage around inside the scooter's cubby hole moving somethings about. Harry could hear things being moved about, and then from the cubby hole, she then removed…an entire TURKEY!'

Both boys' jaws dropped; they were completely and utterly amazed. 'How did you get that turkey inside that small space?' asked Harry looking inside the scooter's cubby hole.

'You'd be surprised what you can get in if you pack carefully,' replied Aunty Dare with a serious look on her face. 'Now, boys, take this plate, (now I'm not sure where that came from) and let's put the turkey onto it and take it to your mummy. She'll need to get it into the oven as soon as possible if she's going to feed us all.'

Harry and Hugo both held the plate very carefully as Aunty Dare placed the turkey onto it. It was quite heavy and they had to concentrate very hard so as not to drop it. Then slowly and very carefully, they all walked together back to the kitchen.

'Mummy, Mummy, Mummy,' the boys shouted excitedly, 'look at what we've got…'

Mrs Alliss just couldn't believe her eyes; in fact, she was so surprised that she dropped the two champagne glasses she was holding for Lady Vix. With catlike reflexes, Lady Vix caught them before they smashed on the kitchen floor.

'Wow, good catch, Vix...' Aunty Dare said, genuinely surprised with Lady Vix's amazing catch.

'Hhhhhow on earth did you get that turkey?' Mrs Alliss asked. Everyone now went very silent.

It would be a tricky thing to explain I think you would all agree, but then Harry said, 'It was a special delivery, Mummy, by a delivery person.' Well, that was a perfect explanation if lacking in some details, but everyone laughed probably more out of relief more than anything else.

'Nicely done, young Harry,' Lady Vix whispered to Harry, 'nicely done.' And she tapped her nose with her index finger to show she was very impressed.

'Dare, is this turkey ready for the oven?' asked Lady Vix.

'Yes, slam it in, it's all set to go,' replied Aunty Dare.

'Oven ready, eh, Dare.'

'Yep,' was the reply.

Now by this time, Mr Alliss had arrived in the kitchen and he saw the turkey as it was being placed inside the oven. To say that he was as amazed as Mrs Alliss was, well, probably a slight exaggeration. He was totally and utterly gobsmacked!

'Don't ask, darling,' Mrs Alliss said to Mr Alliss, 'please, don't ask...'

Chapter Four – Total Fun Day

After the turkey was placed safely in the oven, the whole family went back into the front room to start opening the presents. Then suddenly, there was a "pop" sound which came from the kitchen, like a cork coming out of a bottle. Lady Vix then appeared holding a tray and four glasses on it and a bottle of champagne in the centre. 'There, I told you, Nicola, on the left-hand side of the fridge bottom shelf, you can't miss it.'

Mrs Alliss was totally convinced that there wasn't a bottle of champagne in the fridge, but there was the proof, and Lady Vix certainly didn't bring anything in with her either when she came into the house with her. Still, it was that kind of day, and best not to ask too many questions Mrs Alliss thought to herself.

'Darling,' Aunty Dare said to Mrs Alliss, 'is it all right if Vix and myself both stay over tonight?'

Harry and Hugo were thrilled with that prospect. It would be great to play all those Christmas games with Aunty Dare, and nobody can ever beat Lady Vix, not even their daddy!

'Yes, of course,' said Mrs Alliss, 'the two boys can share their room, that will leave a bedroom spare.

'Oh, that's so kind,' said Lady Vix. 'I'm sure you and Nick will be very comfortable on the sofa. Thank you so much for giving up your bedroom.'

Mr and Mrs Alliss looked at each other and said nothing. It was indeed that sort of day, but they all had a fabulous Christmas day, especially the turkey dinner! It was a very magically day indeed...

Harry and the Scout Camp

Chapter One – Hugo's Scout Camp Idea

'Harry, Harry, Harry…' Hugo shouted out as he was running up the stairs to go into Harry's room. He burst into Harry's bedroom and blurted out, 'Mummy said we're going to scout camp; what do you think about that, Harry…?'

Now Harry was taken a bit by surprise by all this commotion, as he hadn't heard of this scout camp idea before. He was quite happily sitting and reading his football annual when Hugo burst into his room, and now this! It was all a bit new news to him. So, he asked his brother for a bit more information.

'What's this about a scout camp, Hugo?' asked Harry.

'Well, Mummy said that we can go to a scout camp and it will be so much fun. We can sleep in a tent and make our own food and go on explores and much, much, more…' Hugo was definitely very excited with the idea of going on a scout camp. Harry, well, he might not have been quite so keen.

'So will we be living in a tent, Hugo?' quizzed Harry.

'Yes, Harry.'

'How many scouts will be in the tent?'

'Mummy said five or six,' replied Hugo.

Harry thought for a moment; he knew that his brother was very excited but he wasn't so sure. He didn't mind going into his tent in the garden playing with his friends, but after they had all gone home and he had his dinner that his mummy had cooked for him, he would go up to his nice bedroom and lie down on his nice comfortable bed, rest his head on his nice comfortable pillow and have a good night's sleep with Pluto by his side. What's not to like? Then he thought about five other boys sleeping in the same tent as he would be in. It could get a bit smelly especially if they had beans for supper! But he could see that Hugo was very, very excited and he didn't want to disappoint him. Then he could hear more footsteps coming up the stairs. It was his mummy.

'Have you asked Harry now, Hugo, about the scout camp I mean?' asked Mrs Alliss when she came into Harry's room.

'Yes, Mummy, Harry is very excited as well,' replied Hugo.

Now Harry didn't think he said that he was very excited about the scout camp, but sometimes, you just must go with the flow. It's the way it works in families.

Mrs Alliss smiled. 'Good, then I'll organise with Mr Barry the scout master so that we can go and meet the troop at the next fireside meeting in the Scout Hall. It's not far, we can walk to it.'

Well, thought Harry to himself, *Mummy seems very excited with the scout camp idea like Hugo; I wonder what Daddy thinks. I'll ask him.* And with that, he went downstairs to find his daddy.

Harry found Mr Alliss sitting in the front room looking at his train magazines. He noticed that there was a section on Mallard. Less said about that the better thought Harry!

'Daddy, can I ask you a question?' started Harry.

'Of course, Harry, fire away, I'm all ears,' said Mr Alliss.

'What do you think about us going to scout camp?' asked Harry.

'Well, Harry, I think it will be great fun. You'll learn how to read maps and go on adventure trails using a compass,' said Mr Alliss.

'What's a compass?' asked Harry.

'It's a little device that points the way to go; it points to North,' explained Mr Alliss.

'But what if I don't want to go to North, Daddy?'

'Then you'll know which way to go,' said Mr Alliss not sounding very convincing. Mr Alliss didn't really know how a compass worked, "but basically, it's a direction finder you use with a map, but no matter".

Harry just nodded and went back up to his room and read his football annual. He could tell that the decision to go to scout camp had already been made. Well, he thought, it can't be that bad as he knew his friends Bertie and Freddie already go to scout camp. It must be all right…surely!

Chapter Two – The Fireside Scout Hall Meeting

Mrs Alliss was on the phone to the scout master, Mr Barry.

'Yes, Mr Barry…Yes, Mr Barry…Yes, Mr Barry…Yes, Mr Barry…No, Mr Barry…No, Mr Barry…Yes, Mr Barry…Very well, Mr Barry, thank you, Mr Barry, goodbye.'

Now Harry did hear his mummy's conversation with Mr Barry as he was going down the stairs, and his mummy was standing in the hallway making the call. He thought that they didn't say very much. His mummy just said "Yes, Mr Barry" and "No, Mr Barry" and then "Goodbye", so what could they be talking about? Mrs Alliss turned around when she finished her call and saw Harry standing close by her. 'Were you listening to my phone call, Harry?'

'Er, well, err, you were on the phone as I was coming down the stairs, Mummy, I wasn't really listening, honestly, really I wasn't, honestly…'

'All right, Harry, all right,' said Mrs Alliss, 'I know you weren't listening in. I was on the phone to Mr Barry. He told me that the next scout camp meeting is on Thursday this week, so I said that we will come and meet the troop. Mr Barry said that some of your friends are already part of the scout troop so you will know some of the boys already. You'll have to look after Hugo and make sure he's going to be all right and help him make new friends, Harry.'

Harry nodded and said, 'Yes, Mummy.' What else can you say!

'So that's settled then, we'll go this Thursday, and I'm sure we'll have a lovely time. Mr Barry said that they have a nice singsong around the campfire; it will be nice, Harry.' And with that, Mrs Alliss turned around and went back into her kitchen leaving Harry to ponder. He thought to himself that there's always something to do, isn't there. Still, he's the old brother and you always must look after your younger brother. It's the law! He wasn't sure about the singsong either, but he's sure he'll join in. He'd prefer to play football, but you can't have everything! The scout camp, now that's an unplanned adventure, thought Harry, *I wonder what will happen next!*

Thursday came soon enough and Hugo was getting so excited. He thought that they were going camping already. 'Shall I pack my backpack, do I need to take a sleeping bag, did you get any food for me, Mummy?' Hugo just couldn't wait to go.

'Hugo, this is just a fireside chat at the Scout Hall, no one is going away to scout camp yet,' Mrs Alliss explained. Hugo looked very disappointed, but Harry wasn't; he wanted to see the football match on TV when he got home!

When they arrived at the Scout Hall, Mr Barry was there to greet them. 'Hello, Mrs Alliss, so glad that you brought your two boys to the hall. Will you be staying or will you come back and pick them up in an hour or so?' Mr Barry asked.

'I'd thought I'd stay and learn a little bit about what you do at scouts,' said Mrs Alliss.

'Oh, no problem at all, Mrs Alliss, no problem at all. You can listen to our little fireside chat, and perhaps a little singsong to finish off with,' said Mr Barry.

'Do you have a fire in the hall?' asked Harry.

'No, Harry, not a real fire that wouldn't be safe; we just put a lamp on the floor and sit around it and pretend it's a fire; it's great fun, Harry,' explained Mr Barry, 'go inside and have a look around; some of your friends are here already.'

Mrs Alliss made her way into the hall. It was full of posters and tables laid out with ropes with knots that were useful to know about and maps and information about the countryside. So much to take in at once!

Harry was a bit surprised that there were some girls in the hall as well, he wasn't expecting that. Mrs Alliss started to talk to Mr Barry's wife, Debora, so he asked if he and Hugo could go over to have a chat with their friends Bertie and Freddie.

'Hello, Bertie, Hello, Freddie,' said Harry. 'I'm glad you're at this scout meeting, at least we know someone.'

The boys greeted one another. They all knew each other and had played football many times in Harry's garden. 'I didn't know that any girls would be here, Bertie,' said Harry.

'Yes, they have recently joined our troop,' said Freddie. 'They can be a bit bossy at times; they're Mr Barry's nieces so we have to be nice to them.'

'Who is that boy with the long thin legs talking to Mr Barry?' asked Harry.

'That's Jason; he's Mr Barry's son; he bosses us around as well,' said Bertie. Harry looked at Jason. He was very tall with matchstick thin legs that popped out of his baggy shorts. Well, thought Harry, he's not going to boss me around!

'What do we do at these campfire meetings?' asked Hugo.

'Oh, nothing much really; we all must sit around that lantern and Mr Barry just keeps talking and talking. Then we have a singsong. That's not too bad. Mrs Barry plays the keyboard and that's the best bit really,' said Freddie.

'Are you going to the scout camp in two weeks' time, Harry?' Bertie asked. 'Because if you are, can we all be together in one of the tents?'

Well, that was again new news to Harry, he didn't realise it would be quite so soon, but he said yes; what else can you say to your friends!

Well, the campfire meeting went much as Bertie and Freddie explained. Mr Barry did much of the talking. He did mention that the boys were going on the scout camp in two weeks' time and if they could pick who they wanted to share a tent with to please let him know as soon as possible. Harry stood up and told Mr Barry that he would like to share with Freddie, Bertie and Hugo. "Never waste an opportunity," Lady Vix would often say to Harry, so he didn't! Mrs Alliss gave Harry a big smile, and when she did that, she would often light up the room. Lady Vix said that when your mummy smiled, she made some people go wobbly at the knees, and his daddy would say that she's easy on the eye. Harry never understood what any of that meant. Why do grownups have to speak in riddles he thought. Why can't they be more like us children? Everyone understands what we say!

At the end of the meeting, Mr Barry asked if anyone wanted to sing a song. To everyone's amazement, Hugo just stood up and started singing.

Ging gang gooli gooli gooli watcha

Ging gang goo, ging gang goo,

Ging gang gooli gooli gooli watcha

Ging gang goo, ging gang goo,

Hayla – hayla shayla – hayla shayla hayla hoo

Hayla – hayla shayla – hayla shayla hayla hoo

Shally-wally, shally-wally, shally-wally, shally-wally,

Oompah, oompah, oompah.

Well, with that, Mrs Barry got on her keyboard and said, 'Come on, children, all of you now, and again, Hugo, please front the top…'

Ging gang gooli gooli gooli watcha

Ging gang goo, ging gang goo,
Ging gang gooli gooli gooli watcha
Ging gang goo, ging gang goo,
Hayla – hayla shayla – hayla shayla hayla hoo
Hayla – hayla shayla – hayla shayla hayla hoo
Shally-wally, shally-wally, shally-wally, shally-wally,
Oompah, oompah, oompah.

…and all the children kept on singing. Thanks to Hugo, it was a fun evening, after all!

Chapter Three – Off to the Scout Camp

The campfire meeting finished and everyone started to go home. Mr Barry went up to Mrs Alliss and the boys and thanked them for coming. 'Hugo, your singing was just incredible. Thank you for learning that song. It's my favourite; it goes back to when I was a lad of your age and started out in the scouts, thank you. I look forward to seeing you on our campsite adventure,' said Mr Barry.

The Allisses started the short walk back to their home. 'Hugo, that was amazing, when did you learn to sing that song?' asked Mrs Alliss. Hugo just shrugged his shoulders.

'It just came out, Mummy; I'm not really sure,' he said.

'Well, I was very impressed, weren't you, Harry?' said Mrs Alliss.

'Yes, me too…' said Harry wishing that they might just walk a little faster so that he could see the start of the match. Harry was pretty sure that his daddy was already watching it on the TV, as it was Spurs, his favourite team!

Over the next two weeks, Mrs Alliss prepared all the clothes and kit that Harry and Hugo would need to take with them. 'I really don't know how I'm going to get it all into your backpacks,' Mrs Alliss said to Harry.

'Oh, why don't you speak to Aunty Dare, Mummy; she knows everything about packing in a small space,' said Harry helpfully.

'*Roll everything up tightly, Nicola, don't fold,*' advised Aunty Dare. So, Mrs Alliss did and much to her amazement much of the boys' kit and clothes were now safely packed away in their backpacks.

Eventually, the big day arrived and Hugo and Harry stood by the front door ready for Mr Alliss to drive them down to the scout camp. Mr Barry had asked if Mr Alliss could stay over for two nights to help with the cooking and looking after the boys, and of course, he was delighted to help. Mrs Barry was very experienced with all the food catering, so between the two of them, they would make a good team, as we already know that Mr Alliss was a good cook!

When Mrs Alliss saw her two boys all dressed in their smart kit with their backpacks standing by the front door, her little heart jumped a beat. She was going to have to say goodbye to them now and not see them for five whole days! It would be the first time that they would be away from home. It then dawned on her how much she was going to miss her Harry and Hugo. Now Harry could see that his mummy was beginning to get upset and he really hoped that she didn't start to cry, because if she did, Harry would as well. He just couldn't bear seeing his mummy upset. But he didn't want to be upset in front of his younger brother, so he crossed his fingers and hoped that his mummy wouldn't cry.

Luckily, Mr Alliss gave her a hug and she composed herself, and there were no tears, but it was a very close call! The boys got into the family car, waved goodbye to their mummy and Mr Alliss drove off to the campsite.

Mrs Alliss waved back to the boys, closed the front door, went to sit on the bottom step of the stairs, put her head in her hands and cried and cried and cried…

Chapter Four – The Adventure Trek

When they arrived at the scout camp, there were two fields set aside for the scouts. One for the boys which was known as the East Field and one for the girls which was called the West Field. There were some tents already pitched up in the East Field and they had already been set up with the camp beds ready for whichever troop would use them. Harry, Freddie, Bertie and Hugo were joined by Raj, who like Harry and Hugo was also new to the scout troop. Raj was a nice boy and Harry knew him from school. Raj was a very tidy lad, and that was a good thing when you live in a tent, as there wasn't a lot of room inside, even though it looked big on the outside!

When the boys settled into their new tent, Jason came over and told them that he was their scout leader. 'You'll have to do exactly what I tell you to do,' he said, 'otherwise, there will be hell to pay.' Well, Harry was having none of it.

'Don't boss us around, Jason,' Harry burst out.

All the boys looked at each other after Harry had said that. They thought that this could spell trouble, big trouble. Jason went up to Harry to tried to scare him, but Harry didn't flinch. He remembered what Aunty Dare had told him. "Square up to a bully, they are cowards really." So, he did! Now Jason was bigger than Harry so he knew that he could get himself into trouble, but no matter, the deed was done. Jason made as if he was going to tackle Harry, but Harry didn't move, not an inch, or two and a half centimetres if you want it in metric! Jason thought the better of it and backed away. 'Just watch it you, just watch it; I've got my eyes on you now,' he threatened and walked off in a huff.

The boys rallied around Harry and patted him on the back. 'Well done, Harry, he's always bossing us around; it's not fair; it's only because he's Mr Barry's son.' Harry wasn't sure how this would end up, but he was glad that he stood up to Jason. He knew now that Jason had to be a bit more careful when he was dealing with the boys.

After breakfast, the Swallow troop, as they were called, were to go on a trek to Lovely Meadow. They would need to use the map and compass and look out for the Venture trail signs. It would be an easy walk and then they could have a picnic when they arrived. They all had to take a little bit of food with them that Mrs Barry had laid out for them. They also had to take a ground sheet to sit on and a plate, a cup and a spoon. All the food was laid out on a table for the five boys, but Harry thought why was there an extra plate and cup and spoon.

They all packed their backpacks and then stood outside their tent ready for Jason to come and take them on the trek. 'All right, you lot follow me, and no talking,' he said.

'He's a bit grumpy this morning,' Freddie said to Harry, 'must be still sore from you standing up to him like you did.'

'Stop that talking,' shouted Jason, 'or else.'

'Or else what?' shouted back Harry; he was getting the measure of that Jason and he really wasn't going to stand for any of it. Jason turned around and looked at Harry but said nothing and just started to walk a lot faster. Now that was a problem as not all the boys could walk that fast especially with their backpacks being full. They were carrying a lot of stuff as well as the food. Jason's backpack looked quite full as well, but it didn't seem to be giving him any problems; he just walked faster leaving the boys behind him.

It was at the fork in the trail that Harry noticed a sign pointing to Lovely Meadow; it was exactly opposite to the way that Jason was going. Harry shouted out, 'Jason, you're going the wrong way!' But too late, Jason either didn't hear him, or didn't want to hear him and kept on walking the wrong way.

'What shall we do, Harry?' the boys asked.

'Let's catch him up, we must stay together,' said Harry. He knew that if they got split up, that could be very bad. So, the boys started off after Jason. Instead of waiting for the rest of the troop, Jason kept walking on and on. But the problem was he was making so many turnings that they all soon lost their bearings. Even Harry didn't know which way they were going. It was only when they suddenly came up to a large wooded area that Jason stopped. Even he realised he was totally lost now!

When the boys got to where Jason was standing, he wasn't looking the smug boy that he was at the campsite. 'You've got us lost, haven't you, Jason?' said Harry. He was quite cross now as he was thinking about his friends and Hugo and what his mummy had told him, "Look after Hugo."

'It's your fault, Harry, you all should have walked faster,' Jason said.

'No, we couldn't; we're younger than you and can't walk as fast, also our backpacks are heavy,' said Harry. 'Take your packs off, boys, and rest up,' said Harry, and the boys all took their backpacks off and sat on the ground, just glad to rest up. It was already getting a bit late and they were miles away from Lovely Meadow. Harry knew that they were in trouble now, but you must keep your head when these things happen, it will be better all around.

'What's in all your bags, let's see what we have as we might have to stay here a while till someone finds us,' said Harry. So, all the boys emptied their bags. All except Jason, he appeared to be a bit reluctant to do so. 'And you, Jason, what have you got?' asked Harry. Jason didn't move so Harry went up to him. Jason grabbed his backpack, but Harry snatched it out of his hand. It was so light! Harry unzipped it and there was nothing inside it. The troop had been carrying their food and Jason's as well!

They all looked at Jason who now felt very stupid and didn't know what to say or do next. Harry knew that to have another fight with Jason would not be a good thing, so he tried to make the best of the pickle that they were in now.

'We'll have to make camp here and try to get some cover over us. Let's make a fire and try to warm some of the food up.' Harry knew that if the boys were busy, they wouldn't squabble, and this is how he was going to avoid it happening. 'Jason and Bertie, find some sticks we can use to make a tent frame with; we can use the ground sheets to make the tent with. Freddie, you look for some firewood, we can use the paper that Jason had in his backpack to light the fire with. Hugo, you help as well. Raj, we need to make a pan to warm the food up with. It looks like the tins are all beans and there is also some fruit. It's not much, but it will have to do.' Harry was taking charge otherwise everyone would have ended up blaming each other and that would have been bad, really bad.

The boys set about what they were asked to do. Within half an hour, they had the frame of the tent made using the cord to tie the frame together from their backpacks. They made a fire using kindling and the paper that Jason had stuffed into his backpack to make it look as if something was in it. Luckily, Jason did have some matches so they could light it. The tricky bit was finding a pot that they could use to warm all the food up with. Cold beans aren't great, are they! Raj stumbled on a box that had been thrown away by somebody and inside it was a paint pot that had a little wire handle. It hadn't been used so they cleaned it up with a little water they had and placed it in the centre of the fire to warm the beans up in. They were all working as a team now. All their differences were forgotten; they were hungry and they needed somewhere to sleep the night before they were rescued.

The warmed-up beans weren't great, but at least, they had something to eat. The tins of pineapple didn't really stretch that far either. They kept the fire going hoping that the smoke might attract attention and then tried to settle down for the evening as best they could. They were a bit cold and a bit scared, but they kept their spirits up by telling little stories and little jokes. Everyone was trying their best to keep calm. Help will come soon, they told themselves.

Chapter Five – The Rescue

The boys slept as best as they could; they were all very tired after the excitement and drama of the day. It was a full moon and it was surprising how much light that gave, which was good as it would have been even more scary had it been a pitch-black night. During the early hours of the night, Harry was woken by a noise; it sounded like a motor car of some sorts. He woke Jason up and said, 'Jason, I think there's someone coming up the trail; we better check who it is first though.' Jason agreed, they couldn't be sure who was coming, so they made their way to the trail path and waited. They could then see headlights approaching. Jason was sure that it was the police or Mountain Rescue or perhaps a farmer, but Harry just wanted to be sure. Then he saw the outline of something that looked very familiar to him. It was Mr Riggley-Sey's Land Rover! It was quite a distinctive car, as it had an orange bonnet which made it stand out!

'Who is it, Harry?' Jason asked.

'Friends,' replied Harry, 'friends.'

Harry ran out to greet and wave down Mr Riggley-Sey's Land Rover. To his surprise, it was not only Mr Riggley-Sey but Mrs Riggley-Sey and Mr Keith as well who all got out of the car!

When Mrs Riggley-Sey jumped out of the car, she went to open the back of the car and took out some silver blankets and gave one to Harry and one to Jason. 'Put these over you, boys, they'll make you feel warm very quickly. Where are the rest of the boys?' she asked.

'This way,' Harry said, 'follow me.'

Within a few moments, all the boys were woken up and each given a silver blanket that warmed them up. Mrs Riggley-Sey had brought a lot of food with her as well. Hot chocolate, tea, biscuits, sandwiches and much, much, more. The boys got inside the Land Rover to warm themselves up whilst Harry made sure that they all had something to eat and drink.

Mrs Julie Riggley-Sey was an ex-army senior nurse and had been to some major rescue missions in her time. She may look like an old grandmother now but everyone is young once and we all live a life. She knew what to look for when it came to taking charge of a bad situation, and she was amazed how Harry was making sure his boys were all safe. She was very proud of him for someone so young to be doing that!

'How did you find us, Mr Riggley-Sey?' asked Harry.

'Well, it was Mr Keith; he had a hunch and it looks like he was spot on right!'

'Mr Keith, how did you know where we were?' asked Harry.

'Well, that's a very good question, Harry, but it just came to me when I heard that you were lost, and I went over to see Alan and Julie and must have convinced them, because here we all are!'

Harry was amazed as he would have expected the police to find them first. How did Mr Keith know and how did he have this amazing hunch? They were miles away from where they should have walked to and to find them in the dark as well! Then two words came to him. "Aunty Dare".

Chapter Six – Going Home

Mr Keith went to try and get a signal on his mobile phone to ring the rescue team that were looking for the boys. He needed some light to see where he was going so Hugo gave him his torch. After a short while, Mr Keith came back and said that he had managed to call someone from the rescue team and they would arrive in the next hour or so.

'That's an amazing torch, Hugo, that you lent me; the light is so powerful for such a little torch. Where did you get it?'

'It was a Christmas present, Mr Keith,' replied Hugo. That appeared to satisfy Mr Keith as he said nothing else. Perhaps he thought that he might get the same torch as a Christmas present as well thought Hugo!

Eventually, the rescue team arrived in a convoy off road vehicles. The paramedics checked over the boys even though Mrs Riggley-Sey had done a magnificent job looking after them. But rules are rules, so we must observe them. They said afterwards that they were all fine, if a little tired.

The boys were then driven back to the scout camp. It was a very bumpy and uncomfortable drive back to the camp, and Harry was very pleased when they eventually arrived. Mr Alliss greeted his boys and gave them a big hug. Mr Barry asked whether they still wanted to stay to the end of the week or go home with their daddy. Hugo looked at Harry and Harry could tell that Hugo still wanted to stay, so Harry said, 'Yes, we'll stay, Mr Barry.'

Mr Barry was very pleased, as he would have looked bad if all the boys had left the camp, but if Harry and Hugo stayed, then the rest of the boys would stay as well. Jason came up to Harry and said, 'Shake Harry,' and gave out his hand to shake hands with Harry and Hugo.

Both boys took his hand and said, 'Shake Jason,' It was a nice way to make up and be friends again, to an experience that they all had learnt a lot from.

Eventually on the last day, Harry and Hugo packed all their stuff away into their backpacks and said goodbye to everyone. Mrs Barry gave the boys a big hug as a thank you for supporting Mr Barry and his scout camp. He was a good man and meant well.

When they arrived at home, Mrs Alliss ran out of the house and gave Harry and Hugo the biggest hugs ever, and I mean EVER! She did cry but so did the boys, but it really didn't matter anymore.

It was later in the day after Hugo had gone up for a bath that Harry had some time to himself. He went down to his tree and sat on the bench and had a little chat to himself like he sometimes did. He was just sitting there when he felt a leaf or something drop on his head. He went to take if off his hair and found a piece of paper like a little note. It had some writing on it.

Dear Harry, I'm so happy that you got home safely and that Mr Keith found you. I knew that he would. Look after yourself, Harry. Your friend Ethelred.

After Harry had read the note, the paper it was written on just dissolved, as if it was made from dust. It was then that Mrs Alliss walked down the garden to see Harry. She was holding a glass of orange squash for him and sat down beside him.

'I brought you some squash to drink, Harry,' she said.

'Thank you, Mummy.' Then after a pause, Harry asked, 'Do you believe in ghosts?'

'I'm not sure, darling,' she said, 'why do you ask?'

'Oh, nothing really, Mummy,' said Harry.

'Did Ethelred say something to you, Harry?' she asked.

Harry was a bit surprised that his mummy had just said that, she remembered! 'Yes,' said Harry, 'he did.'

'Well, that's good, Harry, it means that your spirits are still together as the friends you are; he'll always look after you,' she said and gave him a hug. Harry felt very happy and contented. *Thank you, Ethelred*, Harry said to himself…

Harry and All at Sea

Chapter One – Planning a Holiday

The Allisses were thinking of their next holiday that they were going to take. There were several different choices for them to make. Harry thought that they could go camping, but after what happened on the scout camp, everyone was a bit surprised that Harry had even suggested it, even Harry was a bit surprised with himself. In any case, Mrs Alliss didn't want to spend two weeks in a tent, particularly if it rained for both weeks! Mr Alliss was all for a walking holiday in France and seeing the beautiful French countryside, but nobody else thought that was a very good idea. It seemed to Harry that it would be a very tiring holiday with all that walking every day. Mrs Alliss thought they should go on a beach holiday, and that seemed to be the best idea so far. Then Hugo said, 'What about a sea cruise?' Well, that surprised everyone; it even surprised Hugo after he had said it!

They looked at the holiday brochures and the cruise liners looked amazing and so huge. Also, the holiday destinations were so varied, and both Mr and Mrs Alliss thought that it was a perfect way to holiday. All the food would be prepared for them, there was no need to find restaurants to eat at the end of the day, and the on-shore day trips looked very interesting. So, the family decided and booked the holiday cruise. It was a three-week cruise and they would be sailing to the Tropics, which when Harry asked what that meant, he was told that it would be very, very hot!

The weeks rolled by till the day arrived for the Alliss family to get ready to go on their cruise. Mrs Alliss was very happy when she found out that there were no restrictions on the amount of luggage she could take. Mrs Alliss did like to dress up in the evenings, so she had a lot and we mean a lot of luggage! So, with the car fully loaded with all their suitcases, Mr Alliss set off to the port ready to board the cruise liner and for them all to start their exciting new holiday.

When Harry saw the ship that they were going to sail in, he couldn't believe how big it was and how tall it was too. It looked like a huge floating building. Waiting in the queue for their tickets to be inspected, Harry noticed the name of the ship.

MV – RETS a SID. Harry asked his mummy if she could explain what that meant.

'Well, I think that MV means Merchant Vessel, but I'm not sure about the rest, Harry, perhaps it's the name of the owner or something,' said Mrs Alliss. Harry didn't feel that that was a very good explanation. Perhaps he'll ask his daddy later, if he finds the time to ask him that is!

Once they got to their cabins, Mrs Alliss started to unpack the suitcases and Harry and Hugo went to explore the ship. They had to wear wrist bands so that if they got lost, the ship's crew would be able to bring them back to their parents. Harry felt he had a very good sense of direction so that would never happen. The boys saw all the lifeboats, the outdoor swimming pools, the mini golf course, the restaurants, the cinema and the theatre where the evening shows would take place and all the shops where he thought that his mummy would be spending some or maybe a lot of her time in.

The family would eat in the ship's restaurants. Harry really liked breakfasts most of all as he could have eggs and bacon and sausages every day, but his mummy wasn't that keen on him doing that. So, Harry had to eat something different every other day, but that wasn't all bad thought Harry.

It was once that the ship had been at sea for a while and they arrived in what was known as the Tropics that the weather started to change suddenly. The clouds got very dark and the wind started to get very, very strong. It all happened so very quickly. Harry and Hugo were on a separate deck to their parents. The wind got so strong that the waves started to crash over the ship. It became very scary. Harry took hold of Hugo and together they tried to make their way back along the deck to the safety of the ship cabins. Then suddenly, this huge wave crashed over the deck they were on and the ship lurched over. The next thing that Harry knew was that they were being thrown from the ship by the waves as the water fell over them. It was so frightening, and Harry found that he was in the sea having been swept overboard! He looked around him and saw that their ship was sailing away from him.

'HELP, HELP...' Harry shouted, but the roar from the sea and wind drowned out his voice. All Harry could see was the big ship sailing away whilst he was on his own in the sea. Harry could swim and knew how to tread water to stay afloat. He started looking for his brother because he knew that Hugo had also been swept overboard with him.

'HUGO, HUGO…' Harry shouted, but he couldn't see anything.

'HARRY, HARRY…' a voice reached out to Harry. Quick as quick, Harry started to swim where he thought the voice was coming from. By some miracle, he saw Hugo's head bobbing in the water just in front of him. 'I'm so tired, Harry,' said Hugo, 'I can't swim much longer, Harry, help me please.' Harry knew that he had only minutes to save his little brother; he looked around and saw what looked like a raft floating in the sea. 'Look, Hugo, there's a raft, we must swim to it; I will help you.' The boys swam together. Having Harry next to him gave Hugo that little bit of extra energy for him to reach the raft. Then with super strength, Harry pushed Hugo up onto the raft. Hugo gasped as he lay on the raft's floor. Harry knew that for the moment they were both safe. If only Aunty Dare was here, he thought, she would save them. Thank Heavens that raft was a raft and not a whale Harry thought to himself. *It's funny how these things pop into your head, Harry*, thought to himself, and it made him smile even though they were now in a desperate place.

Harry swam alongside the raft and tried to push it along, but they were not making any headway. Hugo was worried about his brother as well and said, 'Please get in the raft, Harry, there's enough space; it's too dangerous for you to stay in the water any longer.' So, with a last push and with Hugo pulling him onto the raft as best as he could, Harry managed to climb into the raft. He was also by now getting very, very, tired. The boys then huddled together to keep warm. Then a little miracle happened. Harry saw that the raft had a little compartment marked "RESCUE" in red writing. He pulled at the little door and there the boys discovered a little pack wrapped in plastic with some food and some fresh water as well. They were overjoyed. The food was made up of some dried biscuits and some chocolate for energy. It wasn't much, but it lifted their spirits. They ate the food together, happy that they were both safe and had each other to support themselves.

'Don't worry, Hugo, Mummy and Daddy will never ever give up looking for us. They'll find us. Don't worry, I'll look after you,' said Harry.

'Thank you, Harry,' said Hugo who was now so exhausted that he fell asleep. Both boys drifted in the raft all night long, not knowing what was in store for them. Harry cried to himself. Will anyone save them, will anyone save us, he thought! *Aunty Dare, please help us,* was the last thought that Harry had till he too fell fast asleep next to his brother, exhausted by the day's events.

Chapter Two – The Upset

'I'm very sorry, Mr and Mrs Alliss,' said the ship's captain, 'but this freak weather happened so fast, it caught us all by surprise. It took us a little while to search the ship for your two boys. But now, I have informed the coastguard that they have been swept overboard, and they will start the search in the morning.'

'Why can't they start looking now?' asked Mrs Alliss.

'It's too dark and it would be dangerous for the rescue crew,' explained the captain.

'What about my sons, don't you think it's dangerous for them as well!' Mrs Alliss implored.

'I'm very sorry, but my hands are tied; it's what I have been advised, Mrs Alliss,' said the captain. He understood that both parents were only thinking of their boys, but he had his ship and his passengers to worry about as well. It was a truly awful position to be in for everybody concerned.

Turning to her husband, Mrs Alliss said, 'I will never ever give up looking for our Harry and Hugo.'

'Nor will I, darling, nor will I,' said Mr Alliss. Both parents held each other for strength and quietly said a prayer for their boys.

Chapter Three – The Island

It was morning when Harry woke up. During the night, he had rested his head on the side of the raft, and now, water was going over his head. He was also startled when he felt sand with his hand. He got up with a start when he realised that they had stopped floating and had beached on dry land.

'Hugo, Hugo, wake up, wake up…we're safe,' said Harry trying to wake Hugo.

Both boys sat up and took in the scene that they saw in front of them. A long beach to the left and to the right and dry land in front of them. 'Are we on an island?' asked Hugo. 'Are we now safe?'

'I think that we are, Hugo,' said Harry trying to get up. His legs were very stiff and his little body ached, but he still managed to stand up if a little unsteadily. Holding his hand out, he helped his brother to slowly get up as well. Both boys huddled each other, happy to still be alive and safe.

'Look over there, Hugo, let's walk up the beach to those trees and get out of the sun,' said Harry. Both boys struggled up the beach; they ached all over, but they knew that once out of the hot sun, they will start to feel better. After a while sitting in the cool of the shade of the trees, Hugo said, 'I'm hungry, Harry, do you think we we'll find any food here?'

Harry thought for a moment then he had an idea. Back where the raft had beached itself on the island, he did spot a small pool nearby and he thought that he saw some fish swimming in the pool. If they could catch one of the fish perhaps they could cook it if they build a small fire. There was a lot of drift wood lying on the beach and it all looked very dry, perfect for a campfire.

'Let's build a small fire,' said Harry, 'with the wood that's lying on the beach. Then we'll try and catch a fish in the pool by the raft,' said Harry pointing to where the raft was still lying.

So, the boys collected some drift wood and placed it by where they were sitting. Harry broke some of the wood into smaller pieces and made a campfire ready to be lit. Then the boys went down to the seashore where the raft was beached. They saw the pool that Harry had spoken about and could see some fish swimming in it. But how to catch the fish, it's not that easy is it…!

'How are we going to catch the fish, Harry?' asked Hugo. 'They are quite big and I can't catch them in my hands.'

'I know,' said Harry trying to think of a plan. It was at that point that Hugo suddenly said, 'Look, Harry, I've still got Santa's torch, and look, it still works!'

'That's good, Hugo, but we don't need it now,' said Harry, but Hugo wasn't listening, he went over to the rock pool where the fish were and shone the torch at the pool. Suddenly, one of the fish just jumped out of the pool and landed by Hugo's feet. The two boys couldn't believe what they just saw.

'Well done, Hugo, I think that you have just got us our first meal,' said Harry with glee. The boys took the fish and dragged the raft back as well. They thought that it might make a good shelter if they propped it up with some wood. So, they went back to the shelter of the trees where they had prepared the campfire. They found a large leaf onto which they placed the fish, and then Harry thought how were they going to light the campfire.

'Give me your torch, Hugo, this is just a thought, but let's see if Santa's torch can light the fire as well. It seems to be a magical torch so far, perhaps it can perform another trick for us.' Harry shone the torch onto the wood. At first, nothing happened, but Harry persisted, then slowly they saw little puffs of smoke appearing. Then a small flame started. The boys cheered; they had a fire; they could cook some fish!

Luckily in the little spot that they were sitting in, they heard water and found a small stream. The water was clear and clean so they managed to get a drink as well. Harry cooked the fish as best as he could, trying not to burn the leaf too much, and finally, he said it was ready.

Using a small piece of wood as a fork, Harry tried the fish. It was white and cooked; it tasted good. He gave it to Hugo and the boys took it in turns to feed themselves. It wasn't the best meal they ever had but it was tasty, and when you're hungry, everything tastes pretty good!

'What would we have done without Santa's torch,' Hugo said.

'Yes, that's the best torch ever,' said Harry.

'And it sticks to me like glue all the time,' said Hugo. Both boys just laughed and laughed; they were so relieved that they were on dry land and had some food to eat.

The boy settled down and stayed in the shelter of the trees. The propped-up raft made a good little hut that they could use as a shelter to sleep under. They kept the fire burning as it had started to cool down as the sun eventually set. Then they huddled together to keep warm and fell asleep. It was their first full day on the island. They were alive and safe, but what will tomorrow bring!

Chapter Four – Mission Control

The phone rang. 'Hello, Dare…it's Vix, we've got a Code Red. H1 and H2 are posted missing.'

Dare's heartbeat went up, a Code Red was always a danger signal.

'Do you have any information on a possible location yet, Dare?' Vix asked.

'ST has been activated, that's all I know; currently, we are still working on getting the location,' replied Dare.

Dare then looked at her computer screen, it was two o'clock in the morning. She had been working throughout the night on the posted missing call, now it was a Code Red situation, that means it's critical to locate both H1 and H2. She had fallen asleep for a few minutes just before the phone rang; she was annoyed with herself for doing that!

'Yes, I have more information; it's just coming through now…Position is Modeerf Island, but it needs to be confirmed,' Dare replied.

'Good, will you send a pick-up, Dare, once it's confirmed?'

'Yes.'

'Who?'

'Roy.'

'Roy?…Roy who?' asked Vix.

'Roy Bankstead, ex-RAF, Lightning Pilot, best in the business,' said Dare.

'Hmmm, okay, well, looks like you have got it covered, Dare. Good luck, but keep me posted.' And with that, the phone line went CLICK.

Thank heavens for ST, Santa's Torch, thought Dare…

Chapter Five – Meeting Soraya

'You boys over there, who are you?' the voice rang out to Harry and Hugo. The boys had just woken up, and they turned around to see who was calling them. They look bedraggled, their hair was dirty and all awry, and they both looked very frightened and very hungry.

Soraya came closer to where Harry and Hugo were and she looked at the boys. Her heart went out to them. They looked as if they had been through a very frightening time. Not wishing to frighten the boys anymore, Soraya gently said, 'Don't worry, boys, my name is Soraya and welcome to my island of Modeerf. I saw your smoke and thought I would investigate. I don't know how you did it, but it's a good job you lit that fire, because that's how I found you. Please follow me. It's not too far. I will prepare you some food and some drink. You look hungry and tired. You can also wash yourselves in the waterfall; it's lovely and cleansing.'

'Thank you,' was all the boys had the energy to say. They followed Soraya, just happy that someone somewhere had heard their pleas for help. They walked along the cove until they came across a beach hut sheltering in some trees close to the seashore. Sitting on the soft sand outside the hut, Soraya prepared some drinks for them. Harry wasn't sure what was in the drinks, but it was the best drink ever.

Then Soraya said, 'Let me show you the waterfall. You can have a wash whilst I prepare some food for you; you'll feel so much better.'

They walked together as best as they could, as their little legs were so tired, but soon, they could hear flowing water. Then in an opening through the trees, they saw a small waterfall.

'Get undressed, boys and stand under the waterfall. It's lovely and warm. It will make you feel so much better. I'll take your clothes and wash them. They'll dry quickly in the sun.'

Harry and Hugo looked at each other, and Soraya knew exactly what they were thinking. 'Don't worry, boys, I'll come back for the clothes once you're in the water,' said Soraya protecting their modesty.

The boys were relieved. When Soraya had left them, they got undressed and went into the water. It was lovely and warm, and the waterfall was like a gentle shower. They started to feel so much better as Soraya had said they would.

'Okay, boys, I've left a towel for you each. I'll take your clothes and wash them. Don't worry, take as long as you like; there's no rush.' Soraya picked up the boys' tattered clothes, and from one of the pockets, Hugo's torch fell out. Soraya waved the torch to the boys. Harry immediately jumped up. 'Don't lose that torch please, miss,' he cried out.

'Don't worry, Harry,' Soraya said, 'Santa's torch will be safe with me.'

Harry sat down in the water next to Hugo. 'You know, Hugo, it's a bit of a mystery to me about Santa's torch,' said Harry.

'Why's that Harry?' replied Hugo.

'Well, how did Santa's torch survive being in the water as we were swept overboard, how did it help us to catch that fish, how did it light the fire, how is it that it's always stuck to you like glue, Hugo, and how did Miss know it was Santa's torch, I never told her,' said Harry.

'Nor me!' replied Hugo.

Both boys thought about it for a little while. Then Hugo said, 'It's a mystery, Harry...but it's a nice mystery to have, don't you think?'

Both boys laughed out loud. 'Yes, Hugo, that's a good answer,' said Harry. That really pleased Hugo. It made him feel grown up when Harry agreed with him.

Eventually, the smell of Soraya cooking breakfast reached the boys in the pool. It made them feel very hungry, so they got out of the water, dried themselves with the towels that Soraya had left for them and with the towels wrapped around them walked back to the hut.

'Hello, boys, I thought the smell of the food cooking would make you come to the table,' Soraya said with a smile. The table was full of food. Most of which Harry had never seen in his life. There wasn't any eggs, bacon and sausages and perhaps some toast but there was something called a kebab. Harry wasn't sure about it, but it tasted good. There were lots of dips, and Soraya had made a mango smoothie, which was delicious, and both boys drank every drop. There was some bread that Soraya called Injera. It looked very funny to Harry as it was full of holes, but it tasted very good. There were lots of different fruits on the table as well, which Harry enjoyed especially something called a kiwi fruit. The boys hadn't eaten so much in what seemed like ages and ages, and their tummies were almost fit to burst when they had finished.

'Thank you, miss, that was just lovely,' Harry said after they had finished. Then they chatted about where they came from, how they were swept overboard from the cruise ship and about their parents. Then Soraya told them that she lived on this island on her own as she didn't like people very much, 'They can be so disappointing,' she said, 'but I like you two boys; you are great company for me.' That made the boys very happy. Over the days that followed, the boys found a ball and played on the beach just after the tide had gone out. The sand would be flat and firm to run on, and it wasn't too hot to play either. But by midday, it would get very hot, so they stayed in the hut and watched the sea as it rolled in and out on the shore.

'Do you think anyone will ever rescue us, miss?' asked Harry.

'I wish I could radio for help, Harry, but it stopped working and I'm waiting on the supply launch to come out with the spare parts. But it may still take a few weeks before it comes. I'm so sorry, are you missing your mummy and daddy?' asked Soraya. Both boys nodded and looked very sad.

'Don't worry, boys, I'll look after you till then; you'll be safe with me,' said Soraya.

Chapter Six – The Rescue Pilot

'Hello, this is Yankee Kilo, Kilo, Niner, Niner, Niner, Juliette to Ship MV – RETS a SID, Over.'

'Hello, Yankee, Kilo, Kilo, Niner, Niner, Niner, Juliette, what is your position?'

'Hello, ship MV – RETS a SID we are two minutes away from your Port Beam, Over.'

'Land on Helipad, please proceed, Yankee, Kilo, Kilo, Niner, Niner, Niner, Juliette, Over.'

Roger and Out. The helicopter sped towards the cruise liner.

Mr and Mrs Alliss felt wretched. Mrs Alliss had black rings under her eyes as she hadn't been sleeping at all. She was so upset about Harry and Hugo and not knowing if they were safe or not. Mr Alliss wasn't faring any better either, but they consoled themselves as best as they could. Other passengers on aboard were very kind to them, but they couldn't really give them much comfort. So, they kept themselves in their cabin hardly venturing out. On this morning however for some reason or other, which they both didn't understand, they made their way to the ship's viewing deck. This was a panoramic viewing area where they could see all around them. They could see the helicopter in the distance making its way to the ship. It was a dark midnight blue colour and sparkled like a new pin in the sunshine.

The pilot made a perfect three-point landing on the helipad, and the rotor blades started to slow down as the engine had been shut down.

Flight Lieutenant Archie Bond made the final checks and spoke to his co-pilot, Flight Lieutenant Jasper Lane.

'Okay, Jasper, I'll go and get the cargo. Send out a signal that we are here. Code Eleven please.'

'Yes, skip,' said Jasper.

Archie made his way out of the helicopter to be greeted by the ship's purser. Both men saluted each other as a mark of respect. 'This way, sir,' the ship's purser said. Archie followed the purser. 'They were last spotted in the viewing deck, sir, so I will take you there,' said the purser.

Archie said nothing, he just continued following the purser. Archie cut a dash as he walked along the ship's promenade. The ladies on board were quite smitten by this good-looking pilot with his tanned features and smartly cut blond hair. He looked…hot!

When they both arrived at the viewing deck, Archie immediately recognised Mrs and Mr Alliss. He went straight to them, stood briskly to attention and introduced himself.

Hello, Mr and Mrs Alliss, my name is Flight Lieutenant Archie Bond. I'm from PGR and I've come to take you back to base. We have had a confirmed sighting of your sons Harry and Hugo.'

This was all too much for poor Mrs Alliss who tried to get up and nearly fell over. However, Archie with his superb pilot reflexes caught her immediately and stopped her fall.

'It's not a problem, ma'am, we can take our time,' Archie said gently.

'May I please ask who or what is GPR, and how do you know about our sons Harry and Hugo?' asked a very startled Mr Alliss.

'GPR, stands for Global Pan Rescue, we deal with difficult rescues like your sons being swept overboard on the high seas. It's not easy to locate survivors in such a large space, but the good news is we have, and I have been instructed to bring you back. There will be someone called Aunty Dare to meet you when we arrive,' continued Archie.

'Aunty Dare, Aunty Dare!' Mr Alliss spluttered the words out; he was becoming incredulous. 'How, why, what, where.' He couldn't quite get the words out.

'Not to worry, sir, Commander Dare…I mean Aunty Dare will be on hand to explain absolutely everything, shall we go now?' Archie said. They duly walked out of the ship's viewing area and towards the helipad. Archie and Mr Alliss linked arms with Mrs Alliss to steady her, as they made their way slowly back to the helicopter. Once on board the helicopter, Archie asked Jasper to get Mr and Mrs Alliss comfortable in their seats.

'Can you please put on these helmets?' asked Jasper. 'We must fly by military rules, I'm afraid. But they are quite comfortable and you can also hear what we say on the flight desk and talk to us if you want to. This is the On and Off button,' explained Jasper. Once they were all strapped into their seats, Archie did a quick radio test. 'Can you hear me, Mrs and Mr Alliss?' he said.

'Yes, loud and clear, thank you,' they both said.

'Good, starting engines now, we'll be flying for a few hours, so just relax, have a nap if you like. Tea and Coffee are in the little station by your seats. Please help yourselves. Press "T" for tea and "C" for coffee. There are some sandwiches in the draw in front of you as well. Enjoy the flight, Out.'

Archie pressed the big red starter button and the powerful engine spooled up to full power. The rotors were turning and the helicopter felt alive.

'Yankee Kilo, Kilo, Niner, Niner, Niner, Juliette to MV RETS a SID requesting permission to take off,' asked Archie.

'Permission granted, good luck, Yankee, Kilo, Kilo, Niner, Niner, Niner, Juliette…Out.'

Chapter Seven – Roy Bankstead at Your Service

It was early one morning just after another one of Soraya's lovely breakfasts that she noticed something strange. 'Look, boys, over there; it's a man…walking towards us. Whoever can it be?' she said.

Soraya looked a little bit concerned Harry thought, so he went up and stood next to her. He would protect her. Soraya noticed that and ruffled Harry's hair. 'You're a good and brave boy, Harry,' she said. The man got nearer and nearer. He was wearing something that looked like an overall that Harry's daddy would wear when he was working around the house, not that Mr Alliss liked working around the house mind. Then Harry let out a loud cry…

'ROY…ROY…IT'S ME…HARRY.'

The man stood still, looked up and waved, then walked on and stood in front of Soraya. Standing briskly to attention, he gave a salute.

'Squadron Leader Roy Bankstead, ma'am, hope I didn't startle you with my entrance.'

'No, not at all,' replied Soraya with a bit of relief if we are being honest about it. 'Welcome to my island of Modeerf.'

'Thank you, ma'am, that's very kind of you,' replied Roy.

'Oh, Roy, have you come to rescue us?' Harry cried out; he couldn't contain his excitement any longer. 'I certainly have, young man, and your brother Hugo as well if I'm not mistaken,' said Roy.

'How did you get here?' asked Soraya.

'Flew in, parked up around the cove, ma'am,' said Roy in his very polite manner.

'But there's no runway here on the island,' said Soraya.

'No need, ma'am, seaplane, got floats. Bit of an old girl if you beg my pardon, but she's reliable enough,' said Roy.

'Please, I'm forgetting my manners, would you like a cup of tea and perhaps something to eat?' asked Soraya. 'It must have been a long flight to get to this island.'

'I certainly wouldn't say no; it's been an interesting and, as you rightly said, a long flight,' said Roy.

'Roy, I thought that you would come in the Lightning,' said Harry, who was just overjoyed with seeing Roy.

'Yes, big shame there, old boy,' replied Roy. 'Some trouble with the carburettor or something or so my mechanic told me, but it would have been a bit tricky to land as well.'

'Car-bu-ret-or,' said Harry, 'what's that, Roy?'

'It's a device to supply fuel to the engine,' said Soraya. Now that really impressed Harry, even Roy was impressed.

'You know about your mechanics,' said Roy. 'You have to when you live out here,' she replied.

They all sat down in the cool of the shade and Soraya made them a nice refreshing cup of tea with some biscuits. 'Well, boys, we have been searching for you for a little while now, but finally, we got your position,' said Roy.

'How did you find us, Roy?' asked Harry.

'Oh, it wasn't down to me, some mathematical mumbo jumbo from the boffins back at base as usual, but the long and the short of it is, here I am and we'll soon have you home where you both belong,' said Roy.

Harry didn't understand much of what Roy had just said, except the last bit about being home soon. He was happy with hearing that, as was Hugo.

'What is Roy saying?' Hugo asked.

'Oh, some flying talk, Hugo, I think, I don't understand it either,' said Harry, which in all honesty he didn't!

'I think Miss understands; she keeps nodding her head when Roy speaks,' said Hugo.

'Grown-ups, they always speak funny so that us children don't understand,' Harry replied.

After a while sitting in the cool and having a nice refreshing cup of tea and some lovely biscuits that Soraya had made it was time to go. 'Right, boys, let's be having you. The airplane isn't too far away. Let's walk down to it and be on our way. It's going to be a long journey, best we make a start. Will you be joining us, ma'am?' asked Roy.

'No, but I'll come to see you all off. I'll miss you two boys; you have been great fun here on my little island.' The boys gave Soraya a super squeeze. 'Thank you, miss,' said Harry, 'we would have been lost without you; we'll never ever forget you.'

The little group walked down to the cove where Roy had moored the seaplane. It was bobbing up and down in the gentle swell of the sea. The seaplane was all white but the paint was bleached by the strong sun and looked dull and faded in parts. The airplane looked old, a bit battered and well used. Roy could see that the boys were looking at his airplane and even Soraya looked a little bit worried by its overall appearance and condition.

'Now don't worry what it looks like, boys; it flies straight and true and that's all that matters. It's never ever let me down; it might look a bit battered, but it's got a heart of gold,' he said.

Harry was a touch relieved when he heard that. Soraya, well, she just crossed her fingers. They all had tears in their eyes when they said their goodbyes, even Roy. It was a sad moment for Harry and Hugo. They had become very fond of Soraya and she of them. She had looked after Harry and Hugo as if they were family.

'Right, boys, a quick pre-flight check now, have we got everything? Give yourselves a quick pat down to check…' asked Roy.

Harry patted himself down. Nothing but them; he had nothing when he came to this island! Hugo patted his back pocket. 'My torch,' he cried out, 'my torch, I've lost my torch…'

'Don't worry, Hugo,' said Soraya, 'I said that I would look after it for you, and here it is. You look after it now, Hugo, it's a proper little lifesaver,' said Soraya handing the torch to Hugo. He was so relieved and tucked it into his back pocket after thanking Soraya. The boys and Roy had to wade out to the seaplane; it was moored out in deeper water than the boys had expected so Roy had to put Hugo and then Harry onto his shoulders so that they could board the seaplane. Roy may have looked old, but he was quite strong all the same. Once inside the seaplane, Roy told the boys to put on their radio headsets and strap themselves in their seats.

Over the radio, Roy said, 'It's going to get a little bit bumpy as we start to take off, but don't worry, it's all normal.' With that, Roy started the engine. A great puff of black sooty smoke came out the engine exhausts. 'Don't worry boys, it's normal for the old girl to clear her nostrils,' said Roy.

'Hello, Control, this is Golf, Oscar, Tango, Charlie, Hotel, Alpha ready for take-off,' said Roy over the radio.

'Control to Golf, Oscar, Tango, Charlie, Hotel, Alpha, received. Select course B. Good luck. Over.'

Then Roy swung the seaplane towards the sea and gave it full power. Everything rattled and crashed; it all looked and sounded quite alarming. Water was spraying over the little seaplane and Harry thought that this wasn't going to end up well. Hugo looked frightened as well, and then suddenly, it became quiet again as the seaplane reached for the sky and started to climb into the air.

'Told you,' said Roy, 'it's all bangs and pops on take-off, but she's a good old girl, never ever lets me down. Right, boys, you settle down now. There's some food and drink in the seat side pockets. Have a nap if you like, we've got a long flight ahead of us. Rest up, boys, you're in safe hands now.'

Harry and Hugo looked at each other and both felt that this was the last stage now before they would meet their parents. They knew Roy would get them back somehow or other. They had a little bit to eat and looked out of the plane's windows for a while. The blue sea below looked so calm and tranquil now;

everything seemed very peaceful. Then their eyelids started to get very heavy and they both drifted off into a deep, deep, sleep.

Back on the beach at Modeerf, Soraya had watched the little seaplane disappear off into the distance. Somehow, she always had total faith that Roy would safely take off in that battered old seaplane. But why did she ever think that…!

Chapter Eight – Are We Dreaming?

'Harry, are you awake?' said Hugo tugging at Harry as he slept soundly. Harry opened one eye to see his brother standing in front of him. Then he noticed that Hugo was not just standing in front of him but he was standing in his, Harry's, bedroom!

'What…what's happened, Hugo? I don't understand; where's Roy, where's the seaplane where are we…?' asked Harry looking somewhat alarmed and very confused. Then he heard the voice that he knew and loved.

'Hello, Harry, hello, Hugo, so nice to have you back home.' It was Aunty Dare standing by the bed with her arms outstretched and the biggest smile ever on her face. Even Pluto was wagging his tiny tail so pleased to see the boys back again!

'But, but, but how…Aunty Dare?' asked Harry.

'No matter now, Harry, your mummy and daddy will be here in a moment,' replied Aunty Dare, and sure enough, the bedroom door opened and in rushed Mr and Mrs Alliss. They were simply overjoyed seeing their two sons. There were tears everywhere!

'But Aunty Dare,' asked Mrs Alliss once everyone had composed themselves, 'how on earth did Harry and Hugo end up in their beds without us even knowing, how is any of this possible?'

'Oh, Nicola, don't worry now, sorry about all this, but there has been a bit of a communication nightmare, I'm afraid. Messages didn't go out as instructed, you should have been told; I can't apologise enough. Sometimes you just can't get the staff, Nicola,' said Aunty Dare, 'but the main thing is…you've got your boys back!'

Somehow all those tiny little details didn't really seem to matter anymore…

Chapter Nine – The Press Outside

After all the homecoming celebrations were over, Aunty Dare and Harry were sitting quietly in Harry's bedroom when Aunty Dare spoke. 'Harry, I'm afraid, there is something I need to say to you. There's been a bit of a mess with getting your story out to the Press, so if you look out of your bedroom window, you will see a lot of reporters outside who want to get your story. Problem is we can't say too much. You know how it is, Harry. Need to know basis only. This operation needs to protect its cover.'

Harry nodded; he was following what Aunty Dare was saying right up to the point where she said she had something to tell him, then it all went blank. Going up to the bedroom window, Harry peeked through the curtains and looked outside. There were lots, and I mean lots, of reporters lining Acacia Avenue where the Allisses lived. They all had cameras and microphones, and it looked like a big crowd of people.

'I've asked your mummy and daddy to keep the curtains drawn in the house till they all go, but we two have to go outside and say something otherwise they will never leave, and we can't get our lives back to normal.'

'Can I tell them about Roy and Soraya and the Island of Modeerf and the seaplane and Santa's torch?' asked Harry.

'Hmmm, maybe not too much detail right now, Harry, the less you say the better,' said Aunty Dare.

'All right, let's go,' said Harry, and with that, he ran downstairs and opened the front door, with Aunty Dare now running behind him to catch up. She hadn't expected this reaction from Harry.

'Wait for me, Harry...' Aunty Dare was getting worried that the situation was not in her control any longer, Harry was in charge!

There were more reporters outside than Harry had ever imagined and all the cameras were clicking and lights were flashing as he came out of the house. It was all a bit much Harry thought.

'Harry, Harry, tell us about your rescue,' one reporter asked.

'Well, it's like this—' Aunty Dare started to speak, but Harry put his hand up and interrupted her in mid-flow.

'I would just like to say that I owe my life to my brother Hugo, without whom I would have never survived my ordeal. Thank you, Hugo, and thank you to all of you for coming and seeing us, that's very kind of you. I would now like to spend this time with my family, who I have missed so much. I would also like to thank everyone who helped us and made this rescue possible.' And with that, Harry turned around and went back inside his house, swiftly followed by Aunty Dare, who politely waved to the crowd of reporters as she closed the front door.

'Well done, Harry, that was brilliant,' said Aunty Dare once they were safely back inside the house.

'Actually, Aunty, it's all true, I wouldn't have survived without Hugo…'

'I know Harry, and that's what make you so very special, Harry. Always positive and caring.'

Harry and the Grand Prix Races

Chapter One – The Invitation

'Yes, Aunty Dare…Yes, I will…Yes, I think so…No problem, I will ask him…Yes, I think he'll love to…Nice to speak to you too…Yes, take care…Bye, bye'…CLICK! Mrs Alliss put the telephone receiver down in the hallway. The Alliss household had one of those old-fashioned telephones in their hall which Mrs Alliss bought some time ago when she was in her retro mood. That's a fancy way of saying old fashioned.

'Harry, Harry,' Mrs Alliss called out, 'I would like to speak to you, could you come downstairs please?'

Harry was in his bedroom, reading his favourite book on Formula One motor racing. Harry was very interested in Formula One and liked to memorise all sorts of facts about it, like who won the Drivers' Championship in 1971 (Sir Jackie Stewart). He heard his mummy calling him and wondered what the fuss was all about, so he got up and went to the top of the stairs.

'Yes, Mummy, what is it?' asked Harry.

Mrs Alliss looked at Harry and asked him to come downstairs. They then both went into the front room and sat down together, and Mrs Alliss started…

'I just had a call from your favourite aunty, Harry,' said Mrs Alliss.

'Who is my favourite aunty, Mummy?' replied Harry.

Mrs Alliss gave Harry that knowing look, which said that he knew perfectly well who his favourite aunty was, but Harry persisted. 'Who, Mummy, who…'

'Now are you telling me that I have to say who your favourite aunty is, Harry?' Mrs Alliss said.

Harry was feeling a little bit cheeky and mischievous this morning so, he just looked at his mummy with that sweet innocent look that he did so well.

'I have a lot of aunties, Mummy, so I can't really say who my favourite is, as it may upset the others,' said Harry. He knew that was a good line to take!

'Hmmm, very well, Harry; I will re-phrase that,' said Mrs Alliss. She knew that she wasn't going to win this conversation, so she wisely retreated.

'I've just had a call with Aunty Dare and she would like to invite you to a motor race,' she said.

Harry's face started to beam with excitement. *Bingo*, thought Mrs Alliss, *I've got you now, Harry Alliss.*

'And Mummy, and…what did you say, Mummy, to Aunty Dare I mean?' asked Harry.

It was Mrs Alliss's turn now to be a little bit mischievous. 'Oh, nothing, Harry, I didn't think you would be interested,' she replied.

Harry couldn't believe what his mummy had just said. 'But, but, but, Mummy, I would be very interested to go with Aunty Dare to the motor races…she's my favourite aunty,' said Harry, realising what he had just said. *Oops* he thought to himself!

'Oh,' said Mrs Alliss, 'I see, Harry…' but the time to tease by both needed to stop and they both started to laugh at the little charade they had just played on each other.

'I said that you would love to, Harry,' said Mrs Alliss with a smile, and Harry looked so relieved and happy all at the same time. 'Aunty Dare will send us information about picking you up and taking you to the motor race. It's in two weeks' time. She also said that Hugo can come as well, and you will be able to go out in her racing car onto the track. That should be very exciting, Harry, don't you think!'

Harry was beside himself with excitement. He was happy that Hugo would come as well. 'Will Daddy come as well?' asked Harry.

'No, I don't think he will. Unfortunately, he's got so much on with his work now, so sadly, he may have to miss it. He will be very disappointed, but Lady Vix will be there,' said Mrs Alliss, 'and you'll all have so much fun together.'

'Do you know what car Aunty Dare drives?' asked Harry.

'No, sadly, I don't,' said Mrs Alliss, 'but knowing Aunty Dare, it will be a fast one.'

Gosh, thought Harry, going in a racing car for the very first time and seeing Aunty Dare race, it's going to be so, so, exciting. Harry really couldn't wait.

Chapter Two – Going to the Races

Mrs Alliss was told by Aunty Dare that the pickup for going to the motor race would be 7.00 am on Saturday morning. She was sorry for it being such an early start, but the car needs to be prepared before the racing starts, and she needs to be there early as her mechanics would be working on her car.

So, at seven o'clock on Saturday morning, Lady Vix's black Aston arrived exactly on time. The boys were already waiting outside by their front door and rushed out to greet Aunty Dare and Lady Vix and get into the car.

'What, no goodbye kiss?' said Mrs Alliss to her two boys as she was standing by the front door. Harry looked at Hugo and said, 'Quick as quick, Hugo.' And the boys ran back to their mummy and gave her a goodbye kiss.

'Have fun, boys,' Mrs Alliss said, as she waved to Lady Vix and Aunty Dare in the black Aston. The boys got into the Aston's back seats, and although it was a bit small in the back of the car it was still quite comfortable. With all the goodbyes said, the Aston moved off with that powerful engine noise that it always made. Even Mrs Alliss was impressed by how that Aston sounded as it drove away. It sounded like a powerful animal growl, and it made Mrs Alliss tingle a little.

'So, Harry and Hugo this is the plan,' said Aunty Dare, 'we will now drive to the racing track and go to the pits where my car is being prepared. When the track marshal gives his permission, we will be able to drive the car on the race track, and you will see how it goes. Hugo, sadly you'll have to stay with Lady Vix as unfortunately you are still too young to go onto the track. I'm sorry, but perhaps next year.'

Hugo was a bit disappointed, but he knew that Lady Vix would be fun to stay with. Perhaps she will let him sit in the Aston's driver's seat, he thought to himself. That cheered him up!

When they eventually arrived at the racing track, the place was very busy. Racing cars were being prepared for the races, mechanics were working on their cars with grease and dirt on their faces and hands. There was a lot of noise, with car engines being started up and making such a loud noise that both boys had to cover up their ears. Lady Vix drove up to their garage in the pits. It was Pit Number 8 and sitting outside it was this beautiful racing car, with the number 11 painted on the doors and bonnet.

'Is that your racing car, Aunty Dare?' asked Harry.

'Yes, do you like it, boys?' asked Aunty Dare.

'Oh, yes, it's beautiful,' said Harry.

In fact, it was one of most beautiful cars that Harry had ever seen. It had a long bonnet and it was low and sleek. It had funny wheels which were made from wire. Aunty Dare said they were called wire wheels. Harry had never heard of such a wheel, but all the same, it did look amazing as they glinted in the sunshine. It was a very curvy car and sparkled in a deep red colour.

'What is it?' asked Harry.

'It's a Jaguar E Type,' said Aunty Dare, 'and it's just been finished after a long time spent being repaired; it's hard to believe that it's nearly 60 years old,' continued Aunty Dare.

Now Harry didn't really know what 60 years old really meant, but it sounded like a very long time. '60 years old, wow, that's amazing!' said Harry. He was impressed that something so old could still look so modern all at the same time. Harry could see a mechanic working inside the car; he looked a bit too large to fit comfortably inside it. He was getting quite hot and sweaty as well as he was trying to fix something. Aunty Dare went over to her car to have a chat with her mechanic.

'Hello, Adrian, how's the car now?' asked Aunty Dare.

'Almost ready,' said the mechanic, 'it's running really well now; it's as we say, "On the button", just keep it on the black stuff, ma'am,' he cheekily replied.

'Hmmm,' said Aunty Dare, knowing that Adrian was teasing her but decided not to rise to the bait.

'When you're ready, Adrian, then,' said Aunty Dare as the slightly large mechanic sweated and struggled to get out of the car until he eventually almost fell out of it, right in front of Aunty Dare's feet!

'There you go, Adrian, you're out now, can I help you up?' said Aunty Dare holding her hand out to help him up but with a mischievous smile on her face. That will teach you to tease me she thought!

'Vix, could you find out when we can go on track, please?' called out Aunty Dare.

'Right you are, Dare. Hugo you can sit in the Aston, in the driver's seat if you like. Harry, you come with me,' said Lady Vix. Hugo ran up to the Aston without a second prompting, with the biggest smile that any young boy can raise. Once he stood by the Aston, the driver's door automatically opened for him. Then it gently closed behind him once he was safely inside the car.

'I'll look after Hugo, but he'll be fine in the Aston; he can play with all the Aston's buttons, Vix,' called out Aunty Dare knowing how particular Lady Vix was with her car. She was still feeling a little bit mischievous. 'Don't worry about it, you two,' she said as Lady Vix and Harry made their way to the course marshal's office.

As Harry and Lady Vix walked to the office, Harry started by asking, 'Will it be all right for Hugo to play with all the buttons in the Aston, Lady Vix?'

'Oh, don't worry, Harry, the Aston is Hugo-proof; in fact, it's almost unbreakable.' Now Harry didn't really understand that, but he will in another story!

'Lady Vix,' asked Harry again, 'when the mechanic said to Aunty Dare, "keep it on the black stuff", what did he mean by that?'

'Ah,' said Lady Vix, 'it means keep the car on the racing track. Aunty Dare made a very small error in the last practice session yesterday and went onto the grass, which caused her car to spin. He was just teasing her about it,' said Lady Vix.

'Does Aunty Dare have a lot of spins?' asked Harry.

'No, not really, it was a rare error for her, but it shows that we all can make mistakes sometimes, Harry,' said Lady Vix.

Meanwhile, Hugo was having great fun playing in the Aston. The car was talking to him! He didn't know that it could do that, but it suddenly starting speaking to him after the driver's door closed. 'What would you like to do today, Hugo?' it said and so playtime started…!

When Harry and Lady Vix got to the course marshal's office, Lady Vix went to open the door, only to be rudely brushed aside by some young racing driver who stormed out of the office. He never even apologised, as he so rudely pushed past Lady Vix. Seeing the disturbance, the marshal went up to Lady Vix and apologised. 'I'm terribly sorry, madame, but young Henry there was very upset, as his car has been penalised by the stewards for a rule infringement. He was very cross, but he shouldn't take it out on you, so I am very sorry.' Lady Vix accepted the marshal's apology. It wasn't his fault, but as for young Henry, well, look out, thought Harry. That's not going to end up well, he thought to himself!

'When is the track going to be ready for practice?' asked Lady Vix.

'Oh, in roughly five minutes' time, we will give out an announcement over the loud speakers,' said the marshal, and with that, Lady Vix phoned Aunty Dare to tell her that practice was five minutes away.

'We better get back as quickly as we can, Harry; you'll be going out with Aunty Dare, are you excited?'

Harry was so excited and he could only say one word, 'YEEES!'

Chapter Three – The Practice

'Okay, Harry, put on this overall and crash helmet and make sure that this yellow wrist band is visible as we need to show it before we go onto the track,' said Aunty Dare. 'Get changed in the little room in the pit garage.' Harry went into the garage, his little heart beating with excitement; he's going to get into Aunty Dare's racing car and go on the track!

'Perfect,' said Aunty Dare when Harry came out of the pit garage all dressed in his racing overalls. 'Okay, Harry, let's get into the E Type. Adrian will help you with the seat straps. We have put a slightly smaller seat in the car, so it should be a good fit for you.' Harry sat in the E Type for the very first time, and it felt very comfortable. Then he smelt the petrol, the oil, the smell of rubber from the tyres and the wax used to polish the car, it was a heady smell and he loved it. It made him tremble with excitement. Aunty Dare then got into the driver's seat and put her straps on. She gave Harry the thumbs up sign and Harry responded likewise. Then Aunty Dare's voice came on inside his helmet.

'Right, Harry, we have a two-way radio so you can speak to me whilst we are on the track. This car can be a little bit noisy, so that's why we have a radio. Give me a thumbs up that you can hear me, Harry.' Harry gave a thumbs up with a huge smile on his face.

'Right, ignition,' said Aunty Dare and she reached out to press the starter button in the middle of the E Type's dashboard. The car rocked from side to side whilst the starter motor spun up the engine; it then fired up with an immense sound. The exhaust was spitting and crackling as the engine burst into life. The whole car was alive Harry thought. All the instruments on the dashboard were dancing with their needles showing signs of life. It was amazing and exciting all at the same time, and Harry couldn't wait for Aunty Dare to set off. 'One moment, Harry, we must wait to make sure everything is okay with the car. Adrian is just checking it over and we'll be away.'

Adrian walked around the car and inspected it with his mechanic's trained eye. He was listening to it to make sure it sounded right as well, then he stood in front of the E Type's long bonnet and put his thumb up. They were ready to go! Aunty Dare put the car into gear and it moved forward; it was growling as it set of. When they reached the marshal post to get onto the track, both Aunty Dare and Harry showed their yellow wrist bands. The marshal gave them a thumbs up and Aunty Dare accelerated away onto the track. The car gained speed very quickly and the first corner was upon them in no time at all. The world was moving very, very fast for young Harry. His hands were sweating and his little heart was beating quickly. But Aunty Dare seemed very composed; she was in total control, moving this fast and powerful car with ease, making it look so easy to young Harry. He was spellbound by it all. Could this be happening, could he really be travelling so fast around the race track? Was it possible to be braking so hard for all the corners and then accelerating away with such speed? Was any of this possible? Yes, it was, and it was just wonderful and super exciting!

'Harry,' said Aunty Dare on the radio, 'you're very quiet, is everything okay?' But all Harry could do was to raise his thumb and give Aunty Dare a big smile that said, "Yes, I'm okay, Aunty."

Aunty Dare gave a thumbs up sign back to Harry and carried on. The E Type was just flying down the track now, overtaking lesser cars with ease, but on the final lap, a silver Porsche tried to cut across on the second to last corner when Aunty Dare had the racing line. It was a close call, and it was only because Aunty Dare read the situation that prevented a nasty accident from happening. She allowed the driver through but overtook him on the short straight before the final corner much to the other drivers' annoyance.

The waved chequered flag showed that practice was over as the E Type went past the Start/Finish line. Aunty Dare slowed up gently allowing the E Type to run on as it slowly cooled down from all that racing. 'Well, Harry, how did you enjoy that?' asked Aunty Dare. 'Was it what you were expecting?'

Harry was almost lost for words; he couldn't believe what he had just experienced, but he still managed to say, 'Yes, Aunty, that was fantastic; it was incredible to go so fast. You're an amazing driver.'

The E Type made its way to the pits and stopped outside the Number 8 Pit garage. 'Adrian, could you check over the car. Everything looks good. I couldn't find anything wrong with her. Well done, you've made a really good job of it,' said Aunty Dare.

'No problem, ma'am, you made some good lap times today,' replied Adrian, pleased that his work had been appreciated. Lady Vix and Hugo had been on time keeper duties, timing the E Type over each lap that it did. Hugo thought it was such fun to take the times of the car, after Lady Vix had showed him how to do it. 'Harry, Harry,' cried out Hugo after Harry and Aunty Dare got out of the car, I've got all your lap times. Aunty Dare set the fastest lap on the last lap!'

Chapter Four – The Bad Sport

'Oi, you over there,' came a threatening voice towards where Aunty Dare, Lady Vix and the boys were all standing together, 'what's your game? I had that corner, you made me slow down, I would have had the fastest lap otherwise.'

It was Henry, he was the driver of the Silver Porsche that cut over on the approach to the second to last corner that Aunty Dare was taking.

'I believe I had the racing line,' said Aunty Dare, 'you came up too fast and you wouldn't have made the corner had I not braked; you need to drive with more intelligence.'

'What you saying, lady,' sneered Henry walking right up to Aunty Dare in a very threatening manner, 'it's you who are in the wrong; you shouldn't be racing. Go back to knitting or whatever else it is that you do, but don't come here to block better drivers than you!'

It was at that point that Lady Vix went towards Henry with a very purposeful stride. *Oh, oh,* thought Harry, *this isn't going to end up well.*

'Don't you dare speak to my friend in that tone,' said Lady Vix pushing Henry back with the flat of her hand. It was more powerful than it looked, as Henry felt a fair force on his shoulder where Lady Vix pushed him. He stepped back trying not to lose his balance and embarrass himself in front of all the other drivers, who had now crowded around what appeared to be a very embarrassing scene. *She's a lot more powerful than expected,* thought Henry to himself.

'Perhaps you'd like to apologise, you little twerp,' said Lady Vix, with her eyes blazing with fury. Best not to upset Lady Vix, Harry thought to himself!

Luckily, before the situation got completely out of hand, the course marshal appeared again and intervened to calm things down. Taking Henry aside, the marshal told him to "Cool off" and go back to his pit garage. This is very unbecoming to the sport he told Henry. Be prepared for a serious fine for your actions was the last thing that Henry heard.

Turning to Lady Vix and Aunty Dare, the marshal said, 'Again, I'm very sorry about that unpleasantness; it won't happen again,' he said. 'It's not been your day, ladies, has it?'

'Oh, I'm not so sure about that; it's not been all bad,' said Lady Vix, 'fastest lap isn't a bad result, but thanks for helping though, very kind of you.'

Chapter Five – Angry Henry

Henry walked back to his pit garage with a look of thunder on his face. 'I told you not to mess with them two,' said Debbie his girlfriend. 'They are a force, and you sure found that out the hard way, didn't you?' she continued. 'They're not known as the Nut Crackers for nothing, and in front of all the other drivers as well! What did she call you, "a little twerp", well, you really need to control that temper of yours.'

'Why don't you shut up, Debbie?' Henry snapped back; he really wasn't thinking straight. When you're in a hole, you should stop digging, unfortunately Henry was still digging!

'Don't you dare talk to me like that!' replied Debbie with an angry tone in her voice. Debbie was not a girl that would allow being spoken to like that, and with that, she got up, took her handbag and mobile phone, and stormed off. It really wasn't turning out to be a very good day for Henry!

'Hope you lose…badly,' said Debbie as she made her way out of the pit area. Then turning around one more time and at the top of her voice said, 'Oh, and don't worry, I've got the car's key so no problem, at least I can get home today…'

Chapter Six – Before the Race

'Well, let's have a picnic, the racing isn't for a few hours yet so time for a small snack,' said Aunty Dare. She started to prepare a picnic from the hamper which had been packed in the boot of the Aston. Soon it became quite an impressive spread for just a small snack!

With a nice pot of tea and orange squash for the boys, Aunty Dare called over Adrian and his assistant Barry for a bite to eat as well. They all sat on little deck chairs, which had magically appeared from somewhere inside the pit garage and they all started to tuck in. There was smoked salmon sandwiches, egg sandwiches, ham and cheese sandwiches, tomato and cucumber sandwiches, some sausage rolls and something called Kabanos, which were dried little sausages which Harry liked and little pots of yogurt or chocolate mousse for desserts to finish off with.

They were all chatting about the racing when suddenly Hugo just stood up and said, 'I went to the Moon in the Aston when you let me play in it, Lady Vix. It was amazing, and I saw Space Station 33, Harry, you remember that, don't you?'

Harry was taken a little bit by surprise by what Hugo had just said, but he did remember Space Station 33. It was one of their first big adventures. 'Yes, Hugo, I do,' he replied. 'Did you see Mindy as well?'

'No, Harry, I didn't have enough time for that, but the Moon was amazing; there are so many craters on the surface,' said Hugo. Neither Aunty Dare nor Lady Vix batted an eyelid when Hugo was telling them his little story, but Adrian and Barry were a little bit astonished.

Seeing their confusion, Lady Vix tried to explain, 'Hugo is just explaining a time capsule time continuum vehicle, quite interesting, don't you think?' Adrian and Barry continued making a very good impression of a goldfish, with their mouths opening and closing but not knowing exactly what to say.

'More tea, gents?' Aunty Dare asked. 'It's Darjeeling, quite nice don't you think?'

'Oh,' continued Hugo, 'Lady Vix, did you know that your Aston serves up a Baby Chino and Harry's favourites, sausage rolls!'

'Well, I did tick all the options, Hugo, when I ordered it,' said Lady Vix completely deadpan. Adrian and Barry continued to look astonished, with their mouths wide open, not really knowing what to say.

'Bazza, what sort of Aston is that?' whispered Adrian trying to make sense of what was being said over lunch.

'I'm not sure, Ade, but I think it's an expensive one with all those options!' Adrian looked at his mate and just rolled his eyes and shook his head; he was now completely lost for words!

That's the thing about being with Aunty Dare and Lady Vix, magical stuff happens and it can't always be very easily explained, thought Harry, *but it's always fun and adventurous. They are the best days ever!*

Chapter Seven – The Race

An announcement over the racing track loudspeakers suddenly boomed out. 'Will all competitors please proceed to the Start/Finish line for Race Number 1…thank you.'

'That's us,' said Harry very excitedly.

'Adrian, can you please start up the E Type and get it warmed up?' said Aunty Dare.

'Righto, ma'am,' said Adrian, and he quickly scurried away with Barry to get the car started, scoffing the last sausage roll as he went. Suddenly, the pit area became a beehive of activity. Engines were being started, people were running here, there, and everywhere, and the noise was tremendous! Aunty Dare quickly got into her racing overalls and went over to her car. Everything was happening very quickly now.

'Harry, Hugo, you come with me; we'll watch the race from the grandstand,' said Lady Vix. 'Quickly, boys, otherwise the best seats will be taken.' So, wishing Aunty Dare good luck for the race, they rushed off to try and get some good seats to watch the race from.

Aunty Dare got into her E Type. Everything was very familiar in the car; all the controls were where they should be; it was good to go. Adrian helped do up Aunty Dare's seat straps and then gave the thumbs up sign to show that the car was ready and closed the E Type's door. 'Good luck, ma'am; she's all good,' he said. The E Type moved off to take its place on the starting grid.

Aunty Dare drove out of the pits area and onto the track. She went around the track to the Start/Finish line where she took up her position on the grid. Keeping the engine running, she watched the instruments to make sure everything was in order. Water temperature, oil pressure, volts, fuel. All good and in the green. It was then that she noticed a black E Type that drew up alongside her in the number two position on the grid.

Funny, I thought that there wasn't another E Type in this race, thought Aunty Dare to herself. It wasn't in the last practice that she did with Harry. She looked over to the other car. Its windows were all blacked out, but she could just make out the shape of the driver. This driver was all dressed in black, and with a black visor, it wasn't possible to make out any of the driver's features. It had the number 13 on it. Aunty Dare felt a shiver down her back; she hadn't felt that before, but it was a signal for her to be careful.

All the other cars assembled behind them, until the grid was complete. The course marshal indicated that everything was good for the start. Then the starting grid lights went on, then after a few seconds, they went off, and the race started. Aunty Dare made an exceptionally good start with her E Type accelerating cleanly away picking up speed all the time. Up to the first corner, Aunty Dare was ahead of the pack and took the corner at great speed keeping ahead of the black E Type, which was now keeping station directly behind her but not able to out accelerate or overtake the red E Type.

On and on, the two E Types continued to race each other, with Aunty Dare managing to parry every attempt by the driver in the black E Type to overtake her or out brake her at the corners. It was on the last lap that the black E Type made one last challenge on the second to last corner. He kept his braking till the very last moment but hadn't anticipated that he was travelling too fast to make the corner. He went wide and Aunty Dare had the advantage on the last corner by holding the racing line. The Start/Finish line was ahead. Aunty Dare could see that the marshal with the black and white-chequered flag was in position. The black E Type had recovered and now it was a straight race to the finish along the main straight. Aunty Dare accelerated as hard as she could, her foot was hard down on the floor and the E Type was at its absolute maximum. Every system was at or near breaking point! The heat coming from the engine was intense and noise from the car was at screaming point. The black E Type was so close now that she could almost feel the heat from its engine on her back. It was so tense; the crowd were on their feet holding their breaths to see which car would break and who would finish first. Then the red E Type flashed across the finish line with the black E Type just inches away. Aunty Dare was the victor!

Dare took her foot off the accelerator and let the car slow down, the black E Type drew level with her. The driver had wound down his window and looked across to Dare but made no sign of acknowledgement. He then just followed her into the pit area. It was as they both drove into the pits that the black E Type veered off to the left and went into its pit slot. Dare stopped to try and see who the driver was, but the black E Type just drove straight onto a low loader that already had its ramps down. Once the car was loaded, it was very quickly strapped up and the van towing the low loader with the black E Type drove off. The driver never got out of the car!

'Friend of yours, Dare?' it was Lady Vix with Harry and Hugo both standing by the red E Type with huge grins on their faces.

'Well done, Aunty Dare,' said Harry, 'that was a very exciting race, but who was that driving the black E Type; he very nearly caused an accident out there.'

'That I don't know,' said Aunty Dare, 'but I don't think he's a big fan of mine.'

Chapter Eight – Closing Up

Adrian and Barry were waiting for the red E Type to come into their pit garage. They were clapping as Aunty Dare drove in after her victory parade. 'Well done, ma'am,' said Adrian, 'that was mighty; I really thought that the E Type might say enough on that race down to the finish line, but it all came good.'

'Yes, it did well, very well. Best you check her over, Adrian, though. Thanks to both you and Barry. You really did a great job setting her up for today's race,' she said. The two mechanics were very pleased with what they had achieved today and a win as well. They started to busy themselves getting the E Type loaded up ready to be taken away to their garage where it was kept. They had a lot of stuff to do. Mechanics must work hard; it's not as easy as what a lot of people think it is!

Lady Vix got back into the Aston where Harry and Hugo were already sitting as they waited whilst Aunty Dare got changed. She had been chatting to the course marshal. 'There she is,' called out Harry, 'here she comes.'

Aunty Dare got into the Aston; she appeared somewhat deflated and it wasn't what everyone expected. 'What's the matter, Aunty?' said Harry. 'You don't look very happy.'

'Yes, I know, Harry, I just got a funny message on my mobile,' said Aunty Dare. 'It just said, "The next time, you won't be so lucky." Not very friendly is it!'

'Is that it?' asked Lady Vix.

'Yes, that's it,' said Aunty Dare.

'I spoke to the course marshal whilst we were waiting for you, and I asked him who the driver of the black E Type was. It was a late entrant, and he wasn't sure how he got the Number 2 slot on the grid. The name he used was Mr G. R. Unge. Ring any bells, Dare?' said Lady Vix.

'Hmmm,' said Aunty Dare.

'Hmmm, indeed,' said Lady Vix.

'Are we going to be all right?' asked Harry. he sensed that there was something wrong as both Lady Vix and Aunty Dare were now speaking in code, meaning not for little children's ears. So annoying thought Harry!

'Yes, of course, Harry, we'll always take care of you and Hugo,' replied Lady Vix.

'I was just worried about you, Aunty, and this Unge person,' said Harry.

'Ah, that's so sweet of you, Harry, but don't worry, everything is fine,' said Aunty Dare.

Well, maybe, but Harry thought that this episode may come back again…

Harry and the Mighty Grunge

Chapter One – An Early Morning Start

'Wake up, Harry, wake up,' said Lady Vix to Harry who was fast asleep in his bed. It was two o'clock in the morning and Harry was as normal for this time of night, fast asleep!

'Come on, Harry, wake up, wake up,' implored Lady Vix, by this time shaking Harry quite hard to wake him. 'Aunty Dare has been kidnapped by the Mighty Grunge and only you, Harry, can save her,' said Lady Vix. 'The Mighty Grunge is going to stop the world, Harry. All life as we know it on this planet will stop!'

Harry woke up with a start when he heard that. 'Lady Vix, what are you doing here…?' asked Harry rubbing the sleep from his eyes and looking at Lady Vix, who by this time was looking very seriously at Harry.

'Shh, no time to explain now, I'll tell you more once we get going; now quickly get dressed, Harry. No, second thoughts, stay as you are…in your PJs, we've only got two hours to save the planet and find and save Aunty Dare. Hopefully, you'll be back in bed before your mummy and daddy will ever wake up, just put on a coat and some shoes, quickly, Harry, quick as quick.'

Harry knew that he had to act quickly; he got out of his comfy bed and put on his favourite dinosaur jacket and his lucky trainers. He always scores lots of goals with them, so he thought it would be a good idea to wear them! The two of them then left quietly out of the house, trying not to wake anyone. Funnily enough, even Pluto didn't stir in his basket. Harry thought he hadn't been that quiet!

Lady Vix's gleaming black Aston was parked outside the Alliss's house in the road. It looked fast just standing still thought Harry to himself. Lady Vix opened the car's door and jumped into the driver's seat, Harry ran around to the passenger door and got in. Even before Harry had a chance to put on his seatbelt,

Lady Vix gunned the Aston and the car just shot forward into the night like grease lightning!

'Where's all the traffic, Lady Vix?' asked Harry once he got his breath back. The Aston was making light work of driving through the night. The streets appeared to be deserted!

'The Mighty Grunge is stopping the world, Harry, so everything is either never starting or just stopping; it's a very dangerous situation; we haven't got much time to prevent a catastrophe! Aunty Dare has been kidnapped by the DF, that's the Dark Force and we must save her as well, and you, Harry, are the only one person on the planet who can stop it and save everyone,' said Lady Vix.

'ME…but, but, but, but how?' asked an alarmed Harry. 'What can I do, Lady Vix?'

'Aunty Dare has given you secret powers; you just must find them from within you, Harry. Trust in yourself, and you will find them, I promise you,' said Lady Vix.

'But Aunty Dare is just my aunty, Lady Vix, I've got other aunties as well, you know,' replied Harry. This was all becoming very hard to understand.

'Oh, no, no, no, she's a bit more than that, Harry, you know that by now. She's a Super Being and has been sent to Earth to save it from destruction. Unfortunately, she has now become, how shall I say this, a bit more "human",' said Lady Vix, 'She's adopted you Harry and that's because she really cares about you, well, even loves you Harry…you and your family, you're all very, very special to her.'

Harry was a bit confused but wouldn't anyone! Well, very confused actually and a bit, well, no, not a bit perplexed but very perplexed by all that Lady Vix was telling him. The one thing that made him so happy though was that Aunty Dare loved him, because he loved his Aunty Dare, and that above everything else that Lady Vix had told him tonight meant the world to Harry.

Chapter Two – Finding the Computer

'Where are we driving to?' asked Harry.

'London Tower Bridge. There's a series of tunnels underneath the bridge where the Mighty Grunge has a super computer that is altering the rotation of the planet,' said Lady Vix.

'Gosh,' said Harry; it seemed the only appropriate thing to say. They had made very good progress driving through the deserted streets of old London town. Very soon, Lady Vix was parking up the Aston close to Tower Bridge and they both got out of the car. Running down the steps to the lower level by the bridge, Lady Vix stopped in front of a huge black iron door. 'Here, Harry, this is the door we need to open. Give me Santa's torch please.'

'I haven't brought it with me,' said Harry, 'you never asked me to.'

'Never mind that, look inside your coat pocket,' said Lady Vix.

Harry reached inside his dinosaur coat pocket. Nothing in the left-hand pocket, reaching into his right-hand pocket, he felt something. It was the torch! He quickly gave it to Lady Vix.

'How did that happen, Lady Vix? I didn't put that torch in my pocket. My brother was playing with it last night,' said Harry.

'It will never leave you, Harry, when you are in danger; it's just one of those things,' Lady Vix tried to explain. She then shone the torch upon the large door lock. Slowly, Harry could hear the lock mechanism turning and then the lock releasing. The large door slowly creaked open.

'There, keep hold of it, Harry, it will come in useful again,' said Lady Vix handing the torch back to Harry. They both ran in, Lady Vix running on ahead. *She's running quite fast,* thought Harry, trying to keep up with his little legs running as fast as they were able to. He was so glad he had his lucky trainers on! Eventually, they reached a part of the tunnels where there stood another big door. 'Quick, Harry, the torch!' shouted Lady Vix holding her hand out.

Just at that moment, the Grunge door guards came out of the darkness. They raised something that looked like large water pistols to Harry, and then, they fired at Lady Vix. She immediately fell, moaning in pain. Harry was horrified. 'Lady Vix…' he cried out, 'are you all right…' But there was no sound from her. The guards were now coming directly towards him. Harry couldn't think of anything to do, so in desperation he got out Santa's torch and shone it directly at the guards. The light from the torch bathed the guards with an angry pulsating dark red light, and then much to Harry's surprise, they reared backwards covering their faces trying to escape from the light and ran away into the darkness.

Harry went over to where Lady Vix was lying; she was breathing with difficulty and looked deathly pale. 'Use the torch, Harry,' she whispered, 'use the tor…' then Lady Vix stopped talking.

Harry was frozen with fear for a moment, then he remembered what Lady Vix had just said. "Use the torch, Harry. Use the torch…"

Harry still had the torch in his hand, so he shone it on Lady Vix's face and slowly moved it across her body. Harry continued to do this for a few minutes. All the time, he felt as if Aunty Dare was helping him and telling him what to do. Then the ghostly pale face of Lady Vix started to change, it was becoming pink again. Her body started to twitch and move slightly. *She's alive*, thought Harry, *she's alive*; he was just so relieved. The torch gave out a strange humming noise, but he kept shining it on Lady Vix. Then Lady Vix moved her head and reached out to Harry. 'Help me up, Harry; I'm all right now. That was a very close thing, thank you for saving my life.' And she gave Harry's hand a gentle squeeze.

'It wasn't me; it was Santa's torch; it has magical powers,' said a totally amazed Harry. Who would have thought this would be happening to a young boy like me, thought Harry to himself!

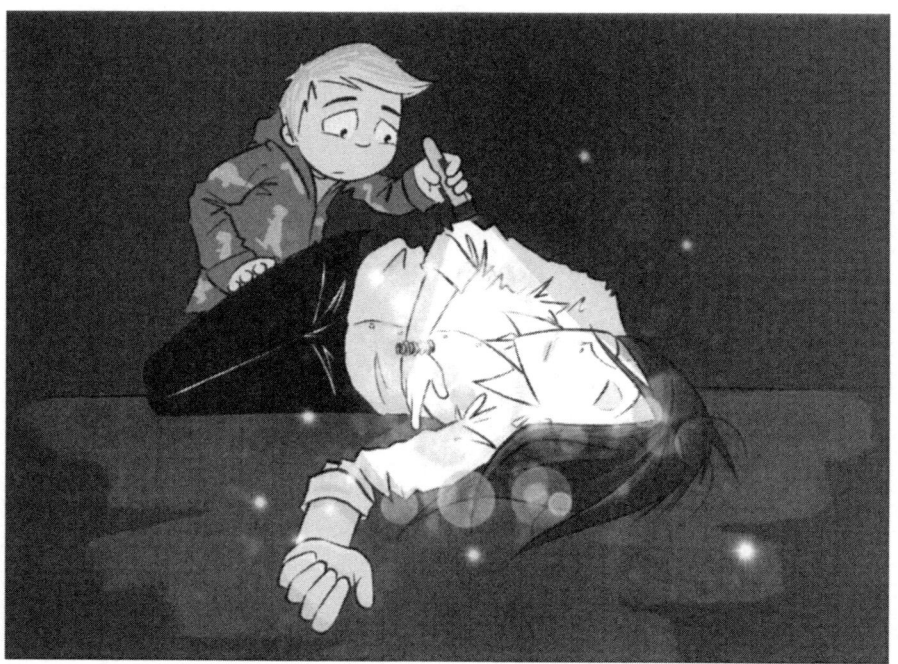

'Ah, Santa's torch very often misunderstood to my way of thinking, but a real lifesaver,' responded Lady Vix with a smile, 'but you must know how to use it, Harry, not everyone knows how to, but you…well, you do!' Harry was just so relieved that Lady Vix was back to her normal self, that he gave her a big hug. Then Lady Vix reacted with shock, as she had just looked at her watch. 'Look at the time, Harry, it's 3.30; we have only got 30 minutes left!'

'What about those horrible guards, Lady Vix?' asked Harry.

'Don't worry, Harry, the light from the torch will have disarmed them; they won't bother us for a while; we still have time to save Aunty Dare and the world, but only just!'

Lady Vix tried to push the door to where the Grunge Computer was, but it was too big and heavy and it didn't budge. 'Go on, Harry, you try,' said Lady Vix. Harry put the flat of his hand against the iron door and pushed against it. The door sprung open!

'There you are, Harry, what did I say, you have super powers, you just needed to find them!' beamed a delighted Lady Vix. Harry, well, he was just totally amazed by it all.

Chapter Three – Where Is Aunty Dare?

They both went inside the computer room. It was a dark and eerie place. It was very cold and had a funny smell to it that Harry hadn't smelt before in his life.

'It's the computer, it's breathing,' Lady Vix said, 'and that's what that smell is if you were wondering, Harry.' All that Harry could see in front of him were rows and rows of lights, all blinking and flashing. They were making patterns with the way they were flashing; it was quite mesmerising but frightening all at the same time. To Harry, the machine was making a breathing noise, a bit like when you have got a heavy cold. It all seemed to make it very scary.

'We have to be brave now, Harry,' said Lady Vix, 'it's now or never, think, Harry, think, what do we have to do to shut down this computer?'

Harry was completely taken aback by what Lady Vix had just said to him. How was he supposed to know how to shut down a gigantic computer like this! *I mean, I'm only a little boy*, thought Harry to himself.

'I really don't know, Lady Vix, I'm really scared,' said Harry, his little body trembling with fear now. Lady Vix went over to Harry and held him gently.

'Listen, Harry, you have the power, you must think. I know it's scary, but I will be with you to the very end. I will never ever leave you. We will both go together whatever happens. I promise you,' said Lady Vix.

That comforted Harry, so he sat down and put his head in his hands and started to think, really, hard like Lady Vix asked him, but all he could think of was playing football with his brother Hugo and Pluto!

Suddenly out of nowhere, Harry stood up and said, 'Remove the pearl green lights but only the pearl green lights. We mustn't touch any of the other lights otherwise the computer program will accelerate and then we will not be able to stop it.'

Lady Vix went up to the machine and looked closely at how it was assembled. 'How do we remove these lights, Harry, they appear to be to part of the machine?'

'They are in individual slots,' said Harry. 'The Yobbermen built it, and they rely on touch to fit and release the light pods from these slots.'

Lady Vix touched only the slots with the pearl green lights to release them but without success; she was not able to slide the lights out. Looking around at Harry, and in desperation as time was now running out, she asked Harry to try. Harry went up to the machine, and with his touch, the pearl green light pods moved outwards and fell into his hand.

'That's it,' yelled Lady Vix, 'quickly now, Harry, we haven't much time left.' Harry ran up and down the machine releasing each light pod where the pearl green light shone, but he couldn't reach the ones that were high up. The computer reached from the floor to the ceiling; it was a vast machine!

'Stand on my shoulders, Harry, to reach the high ones,' said Lady Vix. Harry got up onto Lady Vix's shoulders, unfortunately tearing part of her jacket as he did so. Lady Vix held onto Harry with an iron grip. Coo, she's strong thought Harry!

'I still can't reach all of them; I just need to get up a little bit higher, Lady Vix,' said Harry feeling that they weren't going to make it in time. He now felt a sense of panic. Will they be able to finish the task in time?

'Stand on my head, Harry, don't worry, I'll hold your legs, you won't fall,' said Lady Vix.

'But your lovely hair, Lady Vix, it will be ruined; I don't want to hurt you.'

'Don't worry about that now Harry, this is for Queen and County, the planet, Harry, and Aunty Dare. A girl must make sacrifices…well, sometimes!' Lady Vix said with urgency.

Harry clambered up onto Lady Vix's head. He felt a little bit wobbly at first, but Lady Vix's grip was truly strong! Then moving from left to right, they managed to release the last remaining light pods, and now with just seconds to spare, all the pearl green lights had been pulled out. There, lying on the floor were hundreds of these light pods. They both held their breath…The machine then stopped making its noise. It had stopped breathing!

'I think we may have saved the day, Harry. But where's Dare, we must find her and quickly,' said Lady Vix.

They both stood back from the machine and looked at it. Although it had stopped breathing, it still had this aura of danger and sinister presence. In the darkness, something started to hum. It sounded like something was either moving or opening itself. Harry took his torch out and shone it into the darkness towards the middle of the Mighty Grunge Computer. He could just see a large glass box inside the machine. Inside the box, he could make out a shape. The glass box was slowly moving towards the front of the computer…

'Is it Aunty Dare?' shouted Harry excitedly. They both crossed their fingers and held their breath waiting for the glass box to inch forward towards them. It moved slowly, very slowly; it was a very tense moment, and Harry could feel his legs tremble. Finally, it then stopped, opened a side panel, and tipped out a body…

Chapter Four – The Uncovering

The body wrapped in some kind of cloth tumbled onto the floor and rolled towards were Lady Vix and Harry were standing. They both looked at each other and then at the wrapped body in front of them. Lady Vix knelt and started to unwrapped the body. As she started, it began to wriggle and move about.

'Get this cloth off me,' came a muffled cry from within the cloth, 'get this blooming cloth off me!'

Both Harry and Lady Vix pulled away at the cloth as best they could, till they managed to unravel it. There was a lot of it to unravel! There lying on the ground looking slightly bedraggled was Aunty Dare. She was alive and well, and what joy they both felt.

'Well, better late than never,' said Aunty Dare, having now got up from the floor and brushing the dust off that was clinging to her clothes.

'Well, that's some gratitude for you, Harry,' said Lady Vix to Aunty Dare, 'there we are risking life and limb, we saved her life and all we get is this!'

'You look like something the cat dragged in,' said Aunty Dare looking at Lady Vix with her torn clothes and her immaculate hair all awry. She certainly didn't look the immaculately dressed Lady Vix that we all know and love.

'Well, thanks, Dare…I love you too,' said Lady Vix.

Chapter Five – All Together Now

Harry rushed forward and gave his Aunty Dare the biggest hug ever. 'Oh my, Harry, that's a super squeeze. I do believe you are getting stronger and stronger each day,' said Aunty Dare.

'He's tiptop,' said Lady Vix. 'We really couldn't have done any of this without you, Harry!'

'High praise indeed coming from Lady Vix, high praise indeed,' said Aunty Dare. 'Now, could you pass all those light pods to me that are lying on the floor please. I need to do one more thing before we go and call it a day.' Harry went over and with Lady Vix helping they collected all the light pods and placed them in front of Aunty Dare. There were more than they had first thought, once they saw them all lying in a big heap. Aunty Dare then picked up each light pod one by one, placed it in her hand and crushed them into dust.

'Hmmm, impressive,' said Lady Vix, 'what do you do for an encore, Dare?'

Chapter Six – The Final Part

With all the light pods crushed, Aunty Dare, Harry and Lady Vix walked out of the Mighty Grunge Computer room. 'Give me Santa's torch, Harry, please,' asked Aunty Dare.

Harry handed over the torch and then to his amazement, Aunty Dare started to use it to weld up the steel door of the computer door. 'Look away, you two, I have my dark goggles to protect my eyes,' she said. Santa's torch produced a strong intense beam of light that started to melt the metal of the steel door, welding it shut. 'There, nobody will get in now,' said Aunty Dare once she had finished. 'Now that the master chips have been removed and crushed, the computer will start to self-destruct and eventually turn itself into dust,' said Aunty Dare.

'Will it explode?' asked Harry. Harry was concerned that someone could be hurt if it did.

'No, don't worry, Harry, it's based on Cold Fusion technology so as it will slowly warm up it will break down and turn itself into dust. It won't be a threat anymore,' said Aunty Dare. Harry didn't understand what Cold Fusion technology was, but if Aunty Dare said it was okay, then it must be okay.

'What about those nasty guards that shot and hurt Lady Vix?' asked Harry.

'Oh, don't worry, Harry, now that the pearl light pods have been crushed those guards will start to calcify. They are artificial intelligence AI Robots; they will be rendered harmless soon.'

Harry might have had heard of AI robots, but he wasn't sure about the rest of what Aunty Dare had said. 'What does "calcify" mean?' asked Harry.

'They will now age very quickly and as they do, they will crumble. Not to worry, Harry, it just means that they will no longer be a problem. Simple!' responded Lady Vix. Harry was pleased when he heard that.

'I suppose you'd like me to take you to your hair dresser now, Vix,' said Aunty Dare.

'Do you know what, Dare, I think I could really murder a cup of coffee right now, an espresso if you please,' said Lady Vix, propping up her hair as best she could.

'Right, let's go to Fizzy Lizzy, it's just around the corner from here,' said Aunty Dare.

'But won't it be closed now, it's still very early in the morning,' said Harry.

'It's one of those cafés that are never shut, Harry, even when it's shut, it's open. Well done, Harry, you saved the day, no one else could have done it except you,' said Aunty Dare.

'Yes, well done, Harry,' said Lady Vix, 'what you did today is, well, fantastic. We both owe you everything, and we mean that from the bottom of our hearts.'

With Harry beaming with pride, they walked out into the dark London night air to find the café. Harry thought that Lady Vix and Aunty Dare were the two people he loved the most but probably only after his mummy, daddy, and brother Hugo of course, but before Pluto the dog!

Chapter Seven – Good Morning, Harry, Nice Dream?

Harry woke up and looked at his digital clock, it was 7.30 am. He could smell breakfast being prepared downstairs. The Alliss household always had a full English breakfast on a Sunday morning and Harry loved his eggs and sausages. He put on his dressing gown and went downstairs, with Pluto following.

'Mummy, Mummy, I had an amazing dream last night; it was all about Aunty Dare and Lady Vix; it seemed so real…'

'Oh, good,' replied Mrs Alliss popping her head around from the kitchen into the hallway where Harry was standing, '…because they are both in the front room waiting for you. You can tell them yourself.'

Harry was a bit taken by surprise; he wasn't expecting his aunty and Lady Vix to be here so early in the morning. Was it all a dream?

Then he saw the Black Aston and Aunty Dare's scooter. He popped his head around and looked into the front room. There were Aunty Dare and Lady Vix sitting and chatting on the sofa, both looking, well, just amazing as ever. Lady Vix looked immaculate and Aunty Dare was her happy smiling self.

'Good morning, Harry, so you had a dream last night about us two, come and sit over here and tell us all about it…